A HEART OF MIDNIGHT

Otherworld Academy - Book Five

JENNA WOLFHART

A Heart of Midnight

Book Five of the Otherworld Academy Series

Cover Design by Covers by Juan

❀ Created with Vellum

FOREWORD

This is the second edition of the *Otherworld Academy* series. The original had some flaws that I have long wanted to address. I love these characters, and I truly wanted to do their story justice.

The second edition is an expanded (and much steamier!) volume with a much better ending. Thank you for reading!

CHAPTER 1

BREE

It was a day of celebration, but Bree's heart was full of fear. She clutched the assassin's note tightly to her chest and wondered if she should go straight to Taveon to tell him what Fillan had done. With a quick shake of her head, she reopened the small square of parchment and read the words for the hundredth time.

You and Taveon have won the crown but only because of me.

You owe me, Bree Paine. And I intend to collect on your debt.

Bree crumpled the note into a ball and threw it into the roaring fireplace, watching the edges curl up and turn black. Smoke filled the air, filling her lungs with soot. She would have to tell Taveon about Fillan's note, but not today. There was no telling how he would react. He might decide to call off the coronation completely, believing that he had not won the crown legitimately if Fillan had been the one to take care of all of the champions. And Bree couldn't have him doing something ridiculous as that. Prince Taveon needed to sit on the throne. He needed to rule Underworld. He was the only one she trusted. He would be kind to the fae in not only his realm, but he would also be kind to those she'd left behind.

Taveon wanted to stop the Tithe, the agreement the Dark Fae had made with the Light Fae realm. The agreement to steal innocent humans from their world and transform them into vicious monsters. It was the only way the Dark Fae could get the energy that they needed to survive.

But Bree knew there had to be another way. A way that would not end in so much death. A way that Taveon had sworn he would find.

With a deep breath, she gave a nod to confirm her reasoning with herself. She would tell Taveon exactly what Fillan's note said, but she would do it tomorrow. *After* the coronation. Through their magical bond, Bree could feel excitement and hope rippling toward her. She knew that he would be able to feel her unease, despite how much she tried to keep it bottled up inside. Even though the two of them were inexplicably linked due to the nature of the champion bond, she was able to keep most of her thoughts and feelings to herself...unless she wanted him to hear what was on her mind.

It was a strange sensation, one that she was getting oddly accustomed to. There was a strange kind of comfort in knowing that Taveon was only a thought away. A warmth surrounded her mind and her heart. He was part of her now, as strange as that sounded. And he would be as long as they didn't sever the bond.

Rafferty popped his head around the door to find Bree staring down at the fireplace, her eyes still caught on the charred remnants of Fillan's note. He cocked his head and sized up her expression, but he didn't say a word. Rafe was used to Bree's changing moods by now.

Instead, he let out a low whistle. "You look absolutely breathtaking, Bree. The ceremony is about to start. Are you ready?"

She glanced up at him and smiled, a new kind of warmth spreading through her entire body. Rafe had called her breathtaking, but *he* was the one who could truly steal the air from anyone's lungs. His silver hair curled around his pointed ears, and his eyes flashed with a kind of heat that could make her toes curl. He was tall and lithe, and he moved with a kind of grace that betrayed the truth of who and what he was: a shapeshifting Dark Fae whose raven form soared through the moonlit skies of Underworld. Rafe was part Wilde Fae, but it was impossible to see their orc-like nature reflected in Rafe. He was one of the gentlest, kindest Dark Fae she'd met. A total contrast to the Wild Fae's penchant for vicious violence.

"I'm ready." Bree smiled across the room at him, her eyes drifting to his fitted fighting leathers that stretched across his muscular chest. Even on a day like today, Rafe dressed the part of one of Taveon's warriors. She glanced down at her violet dress with the lacy edges that cut across her chest. "Am I dressed okay? Should I change into my—"

"You look perfect." Rafe strode across the room and held out an arm. "It is an honor to accompany you to the coronation. Every fae in the room will be extremely envious." He gave a wink, and Bree's cheeks filled with heat.

The two of them exited her living quarters and made their way through the castle grounds to join the bustling crowd in the Main Courtyard just inside the front gates. A stage had been erected at the far end where the silver throne had been placed. Usually, the throne sat deep within the Keep in the throne room, but it had been moved outside for the ceremonial day. The Dark Fae believed in each King making his vows for the realm outside and underneath the power of the moonlit skies.

Bree shivered as they strode through the crowd to take their seats toward the front rows. Many of the fae had donned their horns, and strange, gruesome masks had been painted on their faces in varying shades of reds, oranges, and greys. Even after spending weeks inside this castle with these fae, Bree still hadn't grown accustomed to the beastly side they often showed during special occasions. The twisting horns that protruded from their skulls, especially. It was a reminder of exactly where she was and who these fae were. Many of them were full of viciousness. Many of them were dangerous.

She needed to keep up her guard.

Bree and Rafe took a row just behind the previous King's council. Ethne, who had helped get Bree ready, Lord Dagen, whose changing loyalties made Bree's head spin, and Conlan and Branok, both of whom had claimed allegiance to Taveon back before all of this had even begun. She stared at the back of their heads, frowning. Conlan and Branok had seen her meeting with Fillan that day, back during the Silver Moon Ball. And yet, they'd never informed the Prince about it. She couldn't help but wonder why. Taveon had always told her that Fillan did not let anyone see him unless he intended them harm. And yet, not only had Conlan and Branok seen and recognized the fae assassin, but they hadn't even seemed particularly alarmed.

Her thoughts were cut off as the buzzing crowd fell into a sudden hush. In the distance, a low horn echoed through the expansive castle grounds, bouncing off the tall, sharp towers that rose up high all around them. Hooves clattered on the stone ground, starting with a hush and building into a roar.

As if one, every head in the crowd turned to gaze at the front gates of the castle, at the thick iron bars that were being dragged open by two armed guards decked out in red and gold finery.

Two more guards appeared in front of the gates, their black horses trotting down the path. Through the bond, Bree felt the first hint of apprehension from Taveon. Even without seeing him, she knew he was only seconds away from appearing in front of the gates. She sent back her own emotions: encouragement, hope, and something else she couldn't quite name. Something akin to friendship, though that word barely seemed to cover the way she felt about Taveon. Their relationship had been strange from the moment they'd met, and it hadn't gotten any simpler in the weeks she'd spent inside his realm.

First, there had been anger. A hell of a lot of anger. From both sides. Then, there had been a grudging acceptance. Until the anger had taken hold once again. Now, they had a bond that surpassed the magic that connected them together. A strange kind of trust that they could only have after everything they'd gone through.

As Taveon approached the front gates, appearing on his silver stead, Bree couldn't help but feel a blaze of affection toward the Prince. She had tried so hard to keep that affection at arm's length, but it had broken through every wall she'd erected between them.

There was no denying how she felt about him, not anymore, though she barely understood the full depth of it.

Taveon urged his horse forward, coming into full sight of the guests gathered to watch him ascend to the throne. Bree couldn't help but gasp at the flicker of her heart. His dark hair had been smoothed back from his face, highlighting the sharp cheekbones and the commanding curve of his jaw. His eyes were deep pools of pure black, but they somehow glowed underneath the light of the bulbous moon hanging low in the night sky. Underworld was always drenched in darkness. They had no daytime in this realm. But, right now, with the future King striding toward her, Bree felt like a light as bright as the midday sun had suddenly appeared.

As Taveon continued down the pathway that cut through the rows and rows of fae, his gaze caught hers. Something passed between them, a flicker of affection and heat that made every hair on Bree's arms stand on end. And suddenly, she understood what his look meant. Through the bond, she heard it all. Taveon thought that all of this—his coronation, his crown, his throne—was all because Bree had been brave enough to fight as his champion.

But now Bree knew the truth. Fillan had done this. Not her. Taveon's success had nothing to do with Bree. Her heart dropped low in her chest, and she shrunk underneath his beaming gaze. Oh, how she wished she could be the result of that look in his eye. To be the true reason of all that pride. Because that was what it was. He looked proud of her. Proud to have her as his champion. Proud to have her waiting to watch him take his crown.

She blinked back tears and tore her gaze away from Taveon's form, the silver finery barely hiding the tightly-coiled muscles that made him the strongest Dark Fae she'd ever laid eyes on.

"What is wrong, my love?" Rafe leaned close and whispered the words in her ear. She gritted her teeth and turned toward the throne. Rafe didn't need a bond to understand what Bree felt. He could see every emotion written across her face. But she couldn't tell him about Fillan either. Not yet. And definitely not here in front of every single member of the court.

If the wrong fae heard the truth, there was no telling what would happen.

A question-mark came through the bond, but Bree kept her gaze focused ahead instead of behind. Slowly, the Prince approached the stairs, swept his legs over the side of his horse, and gracefully landed on the stone ground. This time, he didn't cast a glance her way, but she could *feel* his attention zeroed in on her, even with his back turned her way.

Everything is fine, she said in a whisper through her mind.

The tension in his shoulders relaxed but only

slightly. He climbed the stairs, coming to a slow stop at the top of the stage. With a deep breath, he turned toward the crowd with his jaw clenched tight. He kept his dark gaze focused on the distant horizon, his chin lifted high. Bree swallowed hard as she stared at him. He was undeniably powerful. Even without his wings spread wide for every eye to see, he carried with him the kind of strength that rippled off his body in waves.

He looked like a Prince. And he looked like a King.

Lord Dagen strode forward from where he'd been waiting in the row just in front of Bree. Taveon had surprised her by choosing the Lord to perform the coronation. The two of them had always been so at odds before now. Prince Taveon had never really trusted Dagen, and the same could be said in reverse. And yet, somehow, they'd finally come together when it truly counted, even though Dagen had once tasked Bree to spy on Taveon.

"Before we get started," Taveon said, clearing his throat after Lord Dagen gave a nod, "I would like to make a short announcement about the future of this realm."

A murmur rippled through the crowd, and Bree furrowed her eyebrows. She'd never attended a coronation before, but she had a pretty good idea that this kind of thing never happened. An announcement?

Prince Taveon held up his hand, a signal for the

crowd to fall silent. "I understand there have been some rumors circling as of late, due do various...circumstances. Some of these rumors are false. However, some of them are very much true."

More murmuring spread through the crowd like wildfire.

"As you all know, each year the Dark Fae and the Light Fae participate in a Tithe intended to provide us with the human energy we need to survive." A pause, Taveon's face growing grave and serious, though that was hardly different to his usual self. "During this process, not only are innocent Light Fae sent away from their families but humans are twisted and deformed into Redcaps. *Innocent* humans. Innocents who then kill more innocents. This is how it has always been, but it is time for a change. I intend to make that change by finding another way for the Dark Fae to draw our energy. And I intend to do away with the Tithe."

The murmurs grew into a roar. A few angry shouts were lobbed at Taveon, but he kept his gaze focused on the distance, and his grave expression never faltered. Instead, he turned to Dagen, gave a nod, and waited for the furor to die down.

Dagen cleared his throat and turned to the crowd, his face pale and his eyebrows cinched tight. "Now that Prince Taveon has spoken his intentions, it is time for the coronation to continue. Everyone, sit down or the Court will find you in disrespect of the proceedings."

At that, silence finally hung heavy over the tense crowd. Prince Taveon had mentioned this part to Bree. Any fae who did not respect the coronation or did anything to disrupt it at all, would be found guilty of treason and thrown straight into the dungeons. It seemed a little extreme to Bree, but she could now see why they had that rule. If they didn't, the whole thing would probably descend into chaos. The Dark Fae were not happy to hear Taveon's plans, and that was putting it lightly.

In the distance, hidden somewhere deep within the castle grounds, a harp began to play a melody that whispered across Bree's exposed skin. It was a soft and soothing kind of tune but one that twanged with melancholy notes. The sound of it dug deep into Bree's bones, and it made her entire body feel as if it was curving toward Taveon and the throne.

Tears filled her eyes, for reasons she did not understand. As she glanced around the gathered crowd, she could see that others were just as moved by the song as she was, despite the fact they'd been two seconds away from fighting only moments ago.

Rafe leaned toward her, his voice rough with emotion. "This is the Song of the Moon Tree. It is always played when a fae becomes King, and it is a song that most here have not heard in centuries. For some, not ever."

Centuries. Bree's heart squeezed tight. The previous King, Prince Taveon's 'father', had ruled these lands for longer than Bree could even comprehend, the lifespan of a Dark Fae never-ending. Unlike Taveon, most of the fae here were *not* immortal. They could die by disease, by poison, by sword. But they would never die of old age, which meant they scarcely ever did. These lands had not been plagued by disease or war in centuries.

Lord Dagen opened up an old wooden trunk that had been brought to the stage by two male fae with dark gray horns. He pulled out the glittering black crown, decorated with row upon row of tiny silver moons. They were bright and bulbous and somehow glowed from within, and the light of the moon glinted across the smooth surface. The sight was dazzling and one that Bree would not soon forget.

Lord Dagen knelt before Taveon, and the swelling music stopped.

"By my commitment to the realm of the Dark Fae, I bring Prince Taveon of the Kavanaugh family before you as the next ruler of our great lands. Taveon, do you make the vow to your peoples?" Lord Dagen's voice was clear and strong, echoing through the hushed crowd.

Taveon gave a slight inclination of his head, and his smooth melodic voice drifted through the courtyard. "I, Taveon Kavanaugh, hereby vow to serve Underworld with all the power, the strength, and the will in my immortal body. I no longer serve myself but the realm as a whole. I give my life to these peoples, here and for always, until the day my body no longer takes a breath."

Bree's heart roared as she watched Taveon lower himself to his knees. The only moment of his life where he would ever have to kneel before anyone else. Lord Dagen stood over him and placed the crown atop his perfect head of black hair. Magic crackled through the courtyard, thick and electric. It buzzed with a new kind of life, a signal of a new age in the realm.

A fresh start.

A better start.

A world where innocents would no longer have to be killed.

For so long, Bree had doubted Taveon. For so long, she'd believed him to be a monster. But she had been so very wrong. Taveon was not the monster he'd wanted her to believe he was. He was brave, kind, and full of the kind of strength that was far greater than any physical demonstration of power.

Lord Dagen leaned over Taveon and slowly placed the crown atop his head. When it made contact, sparks exploded along every inch of her skin. Bree sucked in a deep breath, clutching her hands tight together as an intense dark magic swirled through her veins. It was the realm, gifting Taveon with a raw kind of power, one that would allow him to rule these fae. And she could feel every spark of it through their bond.

After a long moment, Taveon stood on shaky legs to face his new Court. Bree's heart beat madly in her chest. He was now King.

The fae began to disperse after they roared and cheered, and after Dagen made the official announcement. The members of the Court would be eager to get to the Great Hall where a ball would rage all night long to celebrate the arrival of a new King and a new age of the realm.

But just as she turned to join them, Taveon caught her gaze, and he held up a hand. A request.

No, a demand.

He wanted to speak with her.

No doubt he felt her churning emotions. The unease. The fear. And the shame. Bree swallowed hard as she stood and waited for the rest of the fae to disperse. She supposed she would have to tell him about Fillan now, and he sensed that she needed to speak to him alone.

Taveon took a step toward the edge of the stage, and a strange expression flickered across his handsome face. He almost looked...confused. And then a sharp stab went through her gut. Taveon cried out, his eyes rolled into the back of his head, and then he went crashing hard onto the stone ground.

CHAPTER 2

TAVEON

A strange sensation poured through Taveon's body. It was unlike anything he had ever experienced, and it frightened him in a way that little else had during his very long life. It almost felt like…pure, unending pain. The kind of pain that would lead to death.

But that was impossible. Taveon could not be killed. He was immortal. Yes, he could experience pain, but never like this. What he experienced had always been what he imagined a muted version of true pain to be. A dull throb as opposed to the piercing roar that others felt.

Through his bond with Bree, Taveon received nothing but pure fear and panic. But it felt distant, as if viewed through a dark tunnel that had no end in sight. Whatever was happening to him was affecting the bond, a thought that scared him far more than the pain did.

He could not lose his bond to Bree. He'd rather cut off his own arm.

"Taveon," he heard Bree say, though he could no longer tell if she was saying it out loud or in her mind.

"Address the King properly," Conlan said with a snap.

So, out loud then. That was a good sign. At least he was still aware of the world, even if everything surrounding him was nothing but pure darkness.

Bree's soft hand found his, and she squeezed tight as she sent comforting emotions through the bond. "Honestly, you're worrying about how I address him when he's practically comatose? You're worse than he is."

Inwardly, Taveon smiled. That was his champion, through and through. She had never let Taveon get away with anything, and he didn't expect her to let his council members get away with anything either, no matter what his status now was.

"We need to get him inside the Keep and out of sight," Rafe said quietly. "He is still breathing, but he is clearly in some kind of...strange state. The Court should not see him like this. It could cause...issues."

Indeed, Taveon knew Rafe was right, and he couldn't stop the worry from sprouting in his gut. The Court thrived on stability and the knowledge that the King's strength would keep them safe. In Taveon's current state, he could promise them no such thing. Enemies could and *would* take advantage of this.

If they found out.

He sent those thoughts to Bree, and for the first time since the Battle for the Crown, there were barely any barriers between them. She'd let them fall, for once, a fact that brought him more comfort than he wanted to admit.

"Don't worry. We'll fix you," Taveon heard. This time, he was certain the words were sent through the bond instead of being spoken aloud. He could not see anything, but he could picture her face clearly in his mind. Her bright sparkling eyes, her cute little nose, and those shoulders of hers that she liked to throw back as a way to show the world that she was stronger than she looked. Bree was fierce. She didn't necessarily look like it with her petite form, but as soon as anyone saw the full truth of her, it was impossible to think she was anything but one of the strongest fae alive.

Distantly, he could feel Bree watching his body being lifted from the ground and carried out of the courtyard. But he could not feel it himself. It was as if all of his sensations were muted, numbed, as if his body belonged somewhere that his mind currently did not. Sounds were beginning to die away. That little connection he'd had with the world began to fade until every voice was nothing more than distant whispers. If it were not for his bond with Bree, he knew he would have no idea what was happening to him.

"Please don't be scared," Bree said through their bond. "We don't know what happened to you, but we'll fix it."

Taveon wanted to believe her, but as he searched his mind for memories of the past, he could not remember a single time when anything like this had ever happened. It must be some kind of curse. Some witchcraft that had been cast upon his body, a way to stop Prince Taveon from ascending to the throne. But whoever had done this had waited a moment too long. Because the Prince had become the king, even in his weakened state. They just had to keep the realm from finding out before they were able to fix this.

If they were able to fix this.

Taveon sent all of these thoughts into Bree's mind and she stiffened against them. "No," Bree said, her voice insistent. "Don't lose hope. For every spell, there is a counter spell. This realm and Otherworld has always existed on the basis of balance. One thing cannot exist without the other, right?"

"In theory," Taveon said, impressed by how much Bree had learned about his world during the short time that she'd been there. "But just because a counter spell exists, that does not mean that we would ever be able to find it. Whoever did this will be hiding or long gone by now."

"Don't be so sure about that," Bree said, continuing to speak to Taveon through their bond. "One might wonder why someone would put a curse on the Prince during his coronation. One might wonder if that fae wants to become King himself. Or Queen herself. They'll come out of the woodwork to try and claim the throne."

"If this was done by a female, she would not have any reason to believe that she could ever become Queen. Females do not rule Underworld. They never have, and I doubt they ever will."

Taveon could feel Bree bristle against his words. He knew she came from a world where females had become leaders, much more so than they had in Underworld, and he knew that Bree's ferocity made her believe that she could be as strong as any male. And maybe she could be. But Underworld would never accept a female ruler, no matter what kind of curse one had put on the King.

Through their bond, Taveon could see through Bree's eyes. Their group—Conlan, Branok, Dagen, Rafe, and Bree—had entered his chambers now. They carried Taveon's limp body to his bed. Inwardly, Taveon groaned. It pained him that his first day spent as King would be in his bed. This was not how a Dark Fae of Underworld successfully ruled his kingdom. He needed to demonstrate his power and his strength so that the entire realm would fall to their knees before him. Otherwise, he would lose his throne before he even sat on it.

Otherwise, another fae would rise up and try to take his place.

"Bree," he whispered through their bond. "How many of my court members saw what happened to me?"

"Only a few. Most had gone to the Great Hall by that point," she said back with a sad smile. "And the ones who did see what happened understand the severity of the situation and are loyal to you. Besides, Dagen has decided to go to the ball, act like nothing has happened, and say that you became busy with some urgent matter. We'll only be able to keep that ruse up for so long, but it will buy us some time to find the counter spell."

It warmed Taveon's soul that Bree thought so many of the court members were loyal to him, but they were not. They were loyal to his father, and it had only been days since everyone had discovered that Taveon was not even Midas's true-born son. It was naïve to believe that they would be loyal to him just because he'd won the Battle for the Crown. He had never had a chance to show the court his true strength and now he might not ever get that chance.

Bree reached out and took his hand. He swore he could feel her touch through their bond even though he could not feel anything else. She squeezed tight, whispering words of comfort into his ear. He wished he could close his eyes and breathe her in, and he yearned to wrap his arms around her waist, to pull her against his chest. His feelings for Bree had deepened these past weeks, but he had never had a chance to tell her exactly how he felt about her. And now she might never know.

Of course, he knew that she had an inkling of it. As hard as he tried to keep his emotions from traveling down the bond and into her mind and soul, he knew that bits of those thoughts had to reach her. He knew that she could feel the way he felt, or at least a whisper of it.

"I care about you, too, Taveon," she said, sending comfort and hope down the bond.

Yes, Taveon thought to himself. He could feel the truth in her words. She *did* care about him, but in what way? She had never given him any indication that she felt the same way he did. Not just fond of him, but something so much more. A part of him yearned to ask her. A part of him wanted nothing more than for all her walls between them to go crumbling to the ground. But he couldn't ask. Especially not now. Maybe if he made it out of this thing alive, he would wrap his arms around Bree and tell her everything he kept hidden inside the depths of his heart.

That thought alone was enough to make him want to fight his way back.

CHAPTER 3

BREE

Taveon's current state could cause a hell of a lot of trouble in the Court. He'd told Bree as much, though he didn't need to say a word through their bond for her to understand the truth of it. The crown always went to the strongest, fiercest male fae in the realm. That *had* been Taveon. But he certainly wasn't that right now. If word spread...

And word would spread.

Frowning, she pushed open the door to her quarters and strode inside to change into her fighting leathers. It had been a long day, but she yearned to train. To punch something. To curl her hands into the sharp claws of her beast. Anything to work out the tension that clung tightly to her body.

But when her eyes adjusted to the darkness of the

room, she had to bite back a scream. There, in the center of her bed, lay a raven. One with bright red blood pooling around its open beak.

Revulsion build up inside her, and she stumbled away from the bed.

"Hello, Bree Paine," a familiar voice said as a shadow shifted out from the depths of her dark room.

Bree choked out a cry of alarm, though hardly any sound passed between her lips. She stumbled back, eyes widening. Fillan, the assassin, stood before her now. And he was just as she remembered. He still wore his crimson mask and matching jacket, and his glittering sword hung from his waist. Bree's gaze locked on the golden hilt, the one that looked like a lion's roaring mouth. Her heart beat out a frantic rhythm.

Before Fillan could say a word, she took two steps back toward the open door. But just as soon as she turned, she slammed face first into the middle of his massive chest. She let out an oomph and staggered back again, fisting her hands by her sides. How the hell had he managed this little trick?

"If you don't let me go, I swear to the forest, I'll scream so loud that the entire Court will hear," she said through clenched teeth. Inside, she was trembling in fear, but she couldn't very well let the assassin see that she was scared.

"You will not scream because it would be bad for your King if you did."

She raised her eyebrows, her breath catching in her throat. She shouldn't be surprised that Fillan knew about Taveon's state. Still...it left her more than a tad uneasy. "Is that some kind of threat?"

"No." He lifted his shoulders in a shrug. "Just the truth. You need to keep up appearances while he is in his predicament. If the Court discovered that an infamous assassin is sneaking around the castle, in addition to the King being indisposed..."

"You did this. Didn't you?" She wanted to punch the smug fae right in the nose. "You put Taveon in that trance, and you left a dead raven in my bed as some kind of demented warning."

"Alas, I did not." His gaze flicked to the raven on Bree's bed, and he wrinkled his nose in distaste. "That is not my style."

"You're lying." She narrowed her eyes. "Who else would have done something like this? You're clearly after something, and you've been stalking the Prince for weeks."

"The King," he corrected. "And while I may have been 'stalking' as you so politely call it, I cannot take credit for whatever ailment has befallen Taveon. My methods are much more...to the point, shall we say. And I do not wish to see the King dead."

"Well, if it wasn't you, then who was it?" She

glared at him, and then shoved a finger right into his rock hard chest. Bree fought back a wince from the pain that radiated through her hand. "And why the hell are you here?"

"I can only answer one of those questions."

"You *can't* answer both? Or you *won't?*"

A strange smile flickered across the assassin's lips. "I am here because you owe me a debt. And, as I told you in my note, I intend to collect."

"Honestly." She huffed out a breath. "You want to force me to pay you back for something I didn't even ask for? Now, of all times? You say you don't want Taveon dead, but you're certainly not making things easier on him."

"Now, especially," he said quietly. "The realm currently sits on the edge of a very thin blade. One push either way, and it will fall. Which way would you prefer to see it go? Down into the very depths of hell itself or toward the light?"

"I..." Bree furrowed her eyebrows, frustration battling with curiosity. "What the hell are you talking about? You're speaking in riddles."

"I am speaking of Taveon's current state, of the Tithe, of the war coming."

Bree's heart thumped. "What war?"

"The one that will no doubt descend upon your Court if Taveon does not recover."

Bree's face paled, and her heart roared in her ears. While Taveon had warned her what might happen if the Court discovered he was out of commission, he had not mentioned war. The mere thought of it chilled Bree down to her bones.

"It is not *my* Court, Fillan. Not really." She loosed a breath. "But you're right. Are you really telling me that you're here to fix what happened to Taveon?"

A strange smile whispered across his lips. "Do you truly think I am capable of reversing whatever magic has put dear Taveon into this trance? I am afraid I may not be as powerful as you think."

"So, it is magic?" she pressed. "It's not some kind of poison?"

"It could be magic. It could be poison. I cannot say."

Frustration took hold. Fillan was starting to get on Bree's damn nerves. "Honestly, why the hell are you here? Just tell me what you want and get it over with."

Fillan stepped close, bringing with him the scent of burning embers. His chest brushed against hers, and she froze, her lungs filling with timid breaths. "I am surprised you are so eager to rid yourself of me. After our kiss, it seemed as though you quite liked my presence."

Her whole body went taut as warmth began to spread through her neck and cheeks. "Don't be ridiculous. That was merely for show."

Except, even though it had been for show, Bree couldn't deny that she had very much liked her kiss with Fillan. It had been hot and passionate and deliciously dangerous. Shaking her head, she tried to force her feet to step back, but she was rooted to the spot. She didn't understand what was wrong with her. She and Rafe were very much an item, she felt a strange attraction toward Lord Dagen, Taveon was bonded to her mind, her heart, her soul, and now this. It was as if Norah's choice to have a harem had dug its way into Bree's head, and now Bree wanted the very same thing her best friend had.

But that was ridiculous. Norah was a Greater Fae and the ruler of the Light Fae realm. She was magically destined to have four mates. Bree wasn't. Bree was just a human who had become a fae through the Starlight cure. Most fae didn't have multiple mates. In fact, Norah was the first in decades.

Fillan's lips quirked as he gazed down at Bree, their chests still brushing in an intoxicating way. "It is quite difficult for me to believe it was merely for show when my presence unnerves you so."

"Don't be so cocky." And with that, Bree stepped back, though her body scolded her for the move. "I know you didn't come here just to tease me about the kiss. You want me to repay you for what you did, even though I clearly didn't ask you to do a damn thing, much less kill a bunch of champions."

Shivers coursed along her skin. Bree needed to remember exactly what Fillan was. An assassin. And no amount of smooth talking and beautiful looks could change what he did for a living. He killed people. And that was something that Bree could never accept, especially not when he went around saying he did it for her.

"You did not ask aloud, but you wished it all the same." He tucked a finger under her chin, and she shivered. "You desired Taveon to become King, for your own agenda, and yet you did not wish to kill a soul to make it happen, even though that was what was required of you. You volunteered to be his champion, knowing that you would be required to kill others. Do not act as though you are above me."

"No, but I—"

"I need you to look into something for me," he said, his voice suddenly serious. "The answers you find are important to the future of this Court and this realm."

Bree swallowed hard. "Just go ahead and tell me what it is."

"Why does Taveon refuse to spread his wings?"

Bree blinked at him. "I think you must be living under a rock, Fillan. That information became public. Taveon has spent his life refusing to spread his wings because it would have revealed that he isn't King Midas's true-born son."

"Oh, I did not miss that." His eyes glittered, even in the darkness of the room. "But I daresay there is much more to it than that. Even after the reveal of his heritage, or the lack thereof, he has still yet to spread his wings, even at the coronation. Why?"

Bree fumbled for an answer. "Because he doesn't want to use them for intimidation…"

But that wasn't right. Something strange niggled in the back of Bree's mind, like a long forgotten dream from years past. Taveon had used many excuses for his wings since she'd met him, but deep down inside she knew that none of them had been the complete truth. He'd been adamant she not tell a soul that he could not be killed, that he had flown to her side with his silver wings that day he'd brought her to the Dark Fae realm.

And why was that? She was certain the truth lay somewhere inside her mind, but for some reason, it was hidden from her now.

"Why are you asking me to do this? Aren't *you* the spy?"

"I am an assassin. Not a spy." He twisted his lips into a smile. "And you are the one who has the bond with the King. If anyone can get to the truth, it is you."

With a heavy sigh, she crossed her arms over her chest and shook her head. "Sorry, Fillan. I just can't. I refuse to work against Taveon. You can threaten me all you like, but I won't do it."

"I am not asking you to work against him. I am asking you to find out the truth of his nature, for the sake of the realm. If he is who—and what—I believe him to be, then we all might be in grave danger."

Frowning, Bree opened her mouth to ask what he meant by that, but he was gone in a puff of black smoke before she could get out a single word.

CHAPTER 4

DAGEN

Dagen had called together a council meeting after the ball. It had been extremely difficult to get through the night's festivities while keeping the fear and dismay off his face. Every single fae in attendance had been jolly, though he couldn't ignore the whispered conversations that had rippled through the crowd when they'd thought no one was listening.

"Conlan. Branok. Ethne." Dagen nodded at the two Lords and then gave a nod to Ethne in turn. And then he turned to Rafe, who had insisted on joining them, even though he had no place on the council. He was not royalty, nor would he ever be, due to his upbringing. "Rafferty."

The shapeshifting fae crossed his arms over his chest and leaned back in his chair. "Call me Rafe. No need to be all formal in here. A shit storm has broken out in this Court, and we need to get to the bottom of it."

"First things first," Dagen said, wincing at Rafferty's nonchalant way of addressing the council. While Dagen didn't like to think of himself as stuffy, he was certainly one to follow the rules and keep every toe inside the lines. "Most of the fae put on a good show, but there is much unrest in the Court at the present moment, not even considering Taveon's current state. They are...displeased by his announcement."

"Unfortunately for them, they will have to stay displeased," Rafe said with a frown.

Dagen sighed and ran a hand down his face. "You do not understand the ways of the Court, Rafferty. Now is not the time to alienate those who Taveon needs to align himself with."

"He is their ruler. Not their friend." Rafe raised his eyebrows. "That was certainly how Midas preferred to rule. Which you would be very much aware of, being his Hand of the King and all."

"And yet Midas was careful enough to know which branches to bend, which to break, and which to leave firmly attached to the trees."

"Innocent lives are not branches, Lord Dagen," Rafferty said quietly. "We may be Dark Fae, but we are not without our own kind of humanity."

"That may very well be true," Dagen said with a snap. "And I agree that all three realms would be far better off if we put an end to this Tithe. Nevertheless, the Court is displeased. They are concerned by what this might mean for our survival. Until we find a way to reverse whatever has happened to our King, we need to make sure the unrest does not escalate into something much worse than angry whispers."

Rafferty fell silent at that, pressing his lips into a thin line. Finally, Dagen thought with an internal sigh of relief, he understood the gravity of the situation. Because while there could be threats from outside of the castle, if the wrong fae learned of Taveon's condition, the King's announcement could do far worse than that if the council did not keep a handle on it.

The Court itself could break out into war. They could try to take down their new King.

The next morning, Bree met Rafe inside the dungeon-like room that Taveon had dubbed the Dark Fae Academy. He had never come to her bed that night, his hours spent locked up with the council. She had wanted to tell him about the dead raven and all her fears, and she had wanted to feel his arms wrapped protectively around her. But he'd been up all night, making plans with Dagen and the others.

The Academy was dark and dreary, just like most of the rest of the castle, the only window a tiny square at the very top of the domed ceiling. Moon-beams slanted through the thick dust, casting the entire arena into a strange misty light. Even when she'd first come here and had hated being in Under-world, Bree had enjoyed her training sessions with Rafe. But, right now, she wanted to be anywhere other than here. Someone had poisoned the King, and Bree needed to find out who and why.

And she needed to figure out what Fillan was up to before he realized she had no intention of helping him.

"Bree." Rafe whispered out from the darkness, seemingly out of thin air. He did that sometimes. Just like Fillan. Just behind him, two more formless figures strode forward, their shadows dropping away to reveal a female and a male. Both around Bree's age. And both with sharply pointed ears.

Bree widened her eyes. What the hell was this all about?

"As I am sure you recall," Rafe began, gesturing to the two fae who flanked his sides, "Taveon always intended the Academy to expand once he became King. I would like to introduce you to your new fellow trainees."

Bree frowned and flicked her eyes toward the female, whose long fire-red hair was pulled back into a high ponytail to reveal sharp cheekbones, a long, slender neck, and collarbones that could cut deeper than the sharpest blade. She looked unlike any fae that Bree had ever seen, and she was so tall that she was practically twice Bree's height.

"This is Lyra. She is like me in that she is part Wilde Fae and part Dark Fae."

"A shapeshifter as well." Bree gave a nod. She

should have known that any trainee Taveon wanted for this Academy would be a fellow shifter.

"She has spent some time in the Light Fae realm as her Clan kicked her out when she was just a babe."

"Some of the Redcaps took me in," Lyra said, in a deep melodic voice. "They practically raised me."

Bree gave a nod and turned toward the male who was watching the exchange with crossed arms and narrowed eyes. He was the total opposite of Lyra. His hair was dark and cut close to his scalp. Thick and muscular, he was practically a tank. And he was only a couple of inches taller than Bree.

"This is Eurig. He comes from the outposts in the furthest sea down south."

Bree raised her eyebrows and gave Eurig a nod. She knew little about the outposts and next to nothing about the sea that stretched out across most of the realm. From what Taveon had told her, Bree understood the outposts were miles and miles away, and they were governed by their own rulers instead of by Taveon's Court. It was a deal that had been made by Midas, one that formed a strange alliance between them. Midas, of course, had always felt as though the outposts were still *his*, and he merely allowed them to make their own laws as they saw fit.

"I didn't know that the outposts had shapeshifters."

Eurig lifted his eyebrows. "Of course you would

not know. Why would anyone give any thought to us? We are meaningless to your Court."

"No need to get snippy," Bree replied as she crossed her arms over her chest. "I only got here a couple of months ago myself."

"Yes, I know." He flicked his gaze up and down Bree's body as if he were sizing her up, and she couldn't stop the embarrassed heat from spreading across her cheeks. "So, you are the famous champion who 'defeated' all of the Prince's enemies. It certainly was lucky for you that they all happened to end up dead before you were forced to fight them."

Irritation flickered through Bree, and also guilt. He had no idea just how close he'd come to the truth. And she had to make sure he didn't find out. As much as she wished she could trust her new fellow trainees inexplicably, she knew the danger in that.

"Funny, I would have liked a shot at them myself." She smiled. "Or my beast would, really."

"You are just a Redcap." Eurig flicked his hands as if dismissing her shapeshifter form as nothing more than a pesky fly. "And one who was once human. I doubt you could have beaten them all yourself."

"Oh yeah?" Bree raised her eyebrows and took a step closer to the hulking fae. "What do you shapeshift into then? Because I can guarantee it's not more dangerous than my beast."

Eurig's lips twisted into a strange smile. "You will just have to wait and see, now won't you? I would not want to take away the surprise. It is quite...an impressive display of viciousness and strength."

Bree shivered despite herself. Taveon had once told her that there were no other shapeshifters in the realm who were more powerful than Bree. But had he been right? And had he been including the outposts when he'd said that? She knew they had not chosen to partake in the Battle for the Crown because they had their own throne and their own crown to worry about.

Rafe cleared his throat, bringing their attention back onto him. "You will both have a chance to display your strength. To each other and to others as well. As the months here progress, the King will be inviting more and more fae to join us here as trainees, and you will be trained by a variety of instructors."

Bree couldn't help but feel a flicker of disappointment by the news. All along, she'd known Taveon's intentions to grow the Academy into its former glory, but that hadn't stopped her from wanting everything to remain the same. There was something intimate in the way she'd been trained so far. Just the two of them. Working together to fight against the world. She loved the one-on-one with Rafe, though she had to admit that most of that had to do with how she felt about him.

She just had to remember that every step forward

was another step in the right direction. Another step toward ending the Tithe.

"Right," Rafe said with a clap of his hands. "Let us start this session with a shift into your other forms. Bree and Eurig, I believe you should both go at the same time due to the nature of your beasts."

Eurig looked over at Bree and winked. An impossible heat filled her cheeks. "I'll show you mine if you show me yours."

"You can't be serious," she barked back with a roll of her eyes. "That's the lamest pick-up line I've ever heard."

"Oh, I'm not truly coming on to you, Redcap girl," he said with a wink. "If I was, you would have no hope of turning me down."

Okay, so this outposter guy was way more irritating than she'd originally thought. He was more than a little cocky. He seemed to think he was far better than everyone else in the room. And he thought he could get any female he wanted whenever he wanted.

Bree would show him. How? She didn't know.

Rafe stood across the room, frowning at the two of them. He had clearly overheard their entire exchange, and Bree could tell Rafe was not happy about the outposter's flirtations, even if he was using them in jest. Bree was pretty certain that Eurig was just trying to mess with her head and that he had no real interest in turning any sort of seductive charm her way. He probably wanted to show her up during the shift, knowing that her beastly form would far outmatch his.

Bree curled her lips into a smile and focused on the beast within. That would be how she would one-up him. There was no way in hell his shape-shifted form was more impressive than hers.

She went through the motions. Her claws sprouted from her fingertips. Her fangs ripped through her jaws. Her arms bulged and extended, and hair ripped through her skin. At the end of the shift, Bree was left feeling ragged and that old familiar bloodlust sang in her soul. With a curl of her beastly lips, she turned toward Eurig who she could hear panting at her side.

And then her eyes widened. In shock, she took a single step back, her sharp claws scratching against the stone ground.

Eurig shot her a smile full of fangs. She didn't know how to explain what he was. Some kind of lion-like beast, one who was at least a few inches wider and taller than she was. He had golden fur that curled across an impossibly-muscular frame, and his sharp teeth glinted against the dull light of the moon shining through the overhead window.

Bree was something of a wolf. A mangy one. She was strong, and she was powerful, but there was a raw sort of clumsiness she always experienced as a beast. She never felt truly like herself when the wolf took over her body.

Eurig, on the other hand, wore his lion like a second skin. He practically purred as he gracefully strode across the room to stand just before Bree, everything about him rippling with pure and unadulterated power. She felt like an ant compared to his perfect form, one who hadn't had a bath in a hundred years.

Bree curled back her lips and growled.

She swore she heard the lion chuckle. He leaned forward and sniffed, and then he opened his jaw wide to let out a deafening roar. Growling, Bree flicked her tail and turned away from the lion. Enough of this bullshit. She'd had enough. Bree ground her teeth together and forced her body to shift back into her fae form. Rafe was by her side in an instant, handing her a tunic to cover her naked body.

"Well done," Rafe said, his voice tight. "You shifted faster than I have seen you shift in the past."

He did not make a comment about Eurig or point out the fact that he'd practically challenged her to a beastly fight. Instead, Rafe moved over to Lyra's side, coaching her through a shift while Eurig whispered back into his normal body.

When his lion-like form dropped away, he stood before her with a smile. Bree tried not to look at him. He hadn't bothered to grab a tunic from the floor, and his skin glistened from a slight sheen of sweat.

Somehow, that only enhanced the tight look of his muscles, a fact that put Bree more than a tiny bit on edge.

He shot her a wink. "I bet you were not expecting that."

She lifted an eyebrow. "That you'd be an ass? No, I was expecting that."

"There are few fae with shape-shifted forms that can rival yours," he merely said.

Yes, that was true, but she wasn't going to give him the satisfaction of knowing that she thought his lion form was better than her wolf. Instead, she took a step closer to him, swallowing hard at the close proximity to his naked body. And then she slapped him in the face, smiling.

"That's for roaring at me. Maybe next time you'll think twice about challenging a wolf girl to a fight.

CHAPTER 6
RAFFERTY

Rafe had seen Eurig's expression on many a male fae where Bree was concerned. He had seen it on Taveon's face, and he had seen it on Dagen's. It was cautious intrigue, inexplicable fondness, and an attraction that was impossible to ignore. And now Eurig wore it as well, gazing at Bree when he did not think anyone would notice.

While Rafe felt no jealousy or anger toward his King or toward Lord Dagen, the idea of Eurig with Bree made his blood boil in his veins. For one, he was not part of the Court. And two, relations with the outposts had been strained as of late. Rafe understood Taveon's desire to bring one of their shapeshifters into the Academy, but they needed to be careful with their trust. Their secrets needed to stay hidden and protected. And Rafe especially could not trust an outposter with Bree's heart.

Rafe tensed as he glanced Bree's way. He recognized her expression just as he recognized Eurig's. He had seen it on her before. The outposter male was making her flustered, and her eyes had more than once sized up his tightly-coiled muscles. Like many of the fae who lived and worked on the outposts, Eurig was built like the thickest trees found in the Forest of Fireflies.

Eurig caught Rafe staring at the two of them, and he arched an eyebrow, his shoulders rippling as his muscles tensed. "Something wrong, instructor?"

"You need to keep better control," Rafe snapped.

But Rafe wasn't talking about Eurig's control over his shift, and they both knew it.

"More control?" Eurig narrowed his eyes. "I've been shifting since the day I was born."

"It is all emotion. There is too much anger in it," Rafe said. Truth be told, Eurig's shift was strong, but Rafe was still right in his critique. There was a shimmer of anger beneath the surface of Eurig's skin. If he wasn't careful to keep it wrapped up tight, the beast within could go wild with rage. And after seeing exactly what kind of creature the outposter transformed into…losing control was not an option.

"Maybe if you had been raised on the outposts instead of being coddled inside this castle all your life, you would understand what true anger is."

Rafe frowned, and a spark of anger lit a match in his gut. "Do not presume you know anything about me or my life. Or anyone else inside this castle for that matter."

"Honestly," Bree said with an irritated sigh. She strode between them and sent each of the males a sharp look in turn. "I thought we were here to train together, not argue over who had a worse life."

Rafe fell silent and pushed his irritation toward the male fae away. Bree was right. They were here to train. If they were to succeed, they needed to work together instead of against. And it didn't escape his notice that, out of all of them, Bree was probably the one who had experienced the most pain and heartache in her life. She had been viciously attacked by a Redcap when she had been a human, and she'd been transformed into one herself. At the time, the Autumn Court in the Light Fae realm had used her for the beast within her. And then she'd been dragged to the Dark Fae realm against her will, forced to become Taveon's slave.

It was a miracle that she'd agreed to stay.

"Enough of the shifting," Eurig said, grabbing a sword from the weapon rack that hung on the wall just beside the door. He spun the hilt in his hands, wrapping his beefy fingers around the gold. "I propose we have a real fight. One on one. If I win, we call an end to today's training. If you win..." Eurig shrugged.

Rafe narrowed his eyes, torn between walking away and putting this outposter in his place.

"Well, this should be good," Lyra said, crossing her arms over her chest and smiling wide. "It is not every day you get to watch an outposter and a Wilde Fae duke it out."

Rafe heard Bree's wince, though he didn't see it. He was too busy glaring at the outposter to glance her way, but he could guess the expression on her face. Bright eyes dimmed with worry. Jaw clenched tight. Hands twisting together as she paced back and forth across the stone floor.

"There's no need for this, Rafe," Bree said, voice trembling. "You're the instructor. You call the shots here. Not him. And he's a...well, he's a *tank*."

"Alright." Rafe gave a nod and strode over to the weapon's rack where he selected his favorite sword. It was smaller than Eurig's but sharper and much more deadly when used with the right technique. If Bree hadn't said anything, Rafferty would have probably been able to let this go, but he couldn't let Eurig show Rafe up in front of his female. He just couldn't help himself. It was instinctual, something that was hard-wired into the very souls of the Dark Fae. Bree was *his*, and he could not allow another male fae to come across like the winning party.

Rafe held up his sword and shot a glittering smile at Eurig. "We will fight. And when I win, you will agree to never question my training methods again."

"Agreed," Eurig said with a tense smile.

"This is ridiculous," Bree muttered while Lyra clapped her hands.

"One more thing," Rafe said, his voice full of steel. "You will also agree that you will not challenge Bree. Not again. We are all a team here. We will not succeed if we fight amongst ourselves."

Eurig was slower to agree to that one. And Rafe knew why. The outposter enjoyed going toe to toe with Bree, a fact that Rafe understood far better than anyone else. He had felt the same when he'd first met her, and Taveon had kept the dance going far longer than he should. But Rafe would not let some outsider come in and mess with Bree's head.

Finally, Eurig gave a nod. "Agreed."

Swords clashed when the fight between them began. Rafe grunted at the contact, wincing at the strength the outposter showed. Taveon had been wrong to believe this fae was not trained. He had strength, speed, and skill that Rafe had rarely seen, not even in members of the Court.

From an outposter? It was hard to imagine. Those fae lived on wooden platforms erected high above the sea. They lived on fish and fresh sea air, and they did not value swords and steel. How had this male come to be so proficient in fighting?

Rafe got his sword up just in time to block another blow from Eurig's sword. But it was enough force to make him stumble back, and his feet tripped underneath him. Rafe caught his balance just in time, blocking another parry and then swinging his own sword for a forceful blow toward Eurig's legs.

He did not want to hurt the outposter, but Eurig was not holding back. So, neither would he.

Eurig danced away from Rafe's blade as if the weapon was nothing more than a piece of hay. Grunting, Rafe swung again and again, using all of his strength to whip his sword from side to side.

His breathing became ragged, and his movements began to slow. In the back of his mind, Rafe understood what Eurig was doing. It was a technique that Rafe had used himself many a time. Force your opponent to work hard. Tire him out. Let him spend all of his energy. And then make the killing blow when he is far too tired to do a damn thing about it.

But Rafe would not let this outposter get the better of him, not in front of Bree.

So, he made one final attempt to win the fight. Rafe braced his feet on the floor, gritted his teeth, and swung his sword for all he was worth. Eurig caught the blade with his own, and the weapon clattered out of Rafe's hands. His eyes widened as Eurig smiled and lunged forward.

The sharp edge of the sword grazed against Rafe's right leg, and a sharp burst of pain exploded through his core. Rafe dropped to his knees, grasping at the blood now pouring from the brutal wound. And then Eurig's sword flew right at his neck, stopping only an inch short of its mark.

The sharp steel did not cut into Rafe's skin but it might as well have. He felt the damage of the blow nonetheless.

Eurig's deep voice echoed in the cavernous space when he spoke. "Looks like I won. Training is over for the day." The fae pulled back and dropped his sword to the ground before shooting Bree a mischievous smile. Her face was ashen as she blinked at him. "Nice meeting you, Redcap girl. See you tomorrow. If you're lucky."

CHAPTER 7
BREE

Rafe's blood spread across the stone floor, and Bree's stomach tumbled over itself so many times that she felt like she might be sick. She dropped to her knees by his side and pressed her hands against the slick wound. He winced, closing his eyes against the pain. And even though there was no magical bond between them, she swore she could feel the sharp tremors echoing throughout her own body.

"You're an asshole," she shot over her shoulder as Eurig disappeared through the door. Lyra took two steps back, and then quickly followed the outposter out of the Academy's space. Bree huffed and turned back to Rafe, her blood boiling. She couldn't believe that guy. Who did he think he was? The whole point in coming here was to *train*, and yet he'd stabbed his instructor in order to get out of it.

"Do not waste your anger on him," Rafe said through clenched teeth as he handed her a scrap of fabric he'd extracted from his tunic. "He has the typical outposter rage issues. They are brought up to be harsh, bitter, and violent. Taveon knew the risks when he asked Eurig to train here. Besides, I do not think he meant the sword to go so deep."

"If he hates being here so much, then why the hell did he even come?" Bree asked as she fumbled with the fabric. She tied it tightly around Rafe's leg once and then twice, but the blood still fell fast and thick onto the floor.

"Perhaps he volunteered for the same reason you did in the beginning." Rafe shot her a pained smile. "He thought he could make a difference. He wanted to make the realm better for his kind."

"Well, if he really felt that way then he shouldn't be stabbing his instructor!" Bree wanted to throw up her hands, but she was afraid to let go of the cloth. So, she merely let her body tremble with the anger pouring through her like a tidal wave.

Rafe chuckled. "If I recall correctly, you did something quite similar. Or have you already forgotten that you stabbed Taveon on your first day here?"

Bree's heart clenched tight. How could she forget?

"Yeah, but." Bree frowned. "That was way different and you know it."

"Perhaps. Perhaps not." Rafe groaned as he sat up on his elbows. "Bree, I am afraid this wound is going to need far more than just a bandage. I would ask you to take me to Taveon, but…"

But Taveon was in much worse shape than Rafe was in this moment. That said…a lightbulb went off over Bree's head.

"You always ask for Taveon when you're wounded. Why is that, Rafe?"

Rafe was silent for once. He pressed his lips tightly together and glanced away. Even after everything that had happened, the two of them were still keeping something from Bree. Whatever it was linked back to all their other hidden secrets. Taveon's silver wings. Taveon's immortality.

"You might as well go ahead and tell me," she said, pressing her lips together. "I've already figured it out anyway."

Rafe's face paled. "You have figured out Taveon's secret?"

"So, he *does* have a secret? I knew it." She began ticking off the evidence on her fingers. "He has silver wings. He cannot be killed. And he has some kind of healing powers, which is why you keep asking for him when you're hurt."

Rafe flicked his eyes to the open door, and he dropped his voice to a low growl. "Careful, Bree."

"They're gone," Bree said, and then let a beat pass. "So, it's true. Taveon can heal people."

Rafe let out a long sigh. "He can heal fae, yes. But it is best if you keep that information to yourself."

"When are you two finally going to trust me enough to tell me the truth about him? When are you going to explain to me what all of this means?" Bree fought the urge to shove up from the floor and curl her hands into fists. If Rafe wasn't so hurt, she would, but she wouldn't leave his side now. Despite how frustrated she felt about all of his secrets.

"Truthfully, I assumed that you already knew, Bree," Rafe said, wincing as he attempted to stand. Bree grabbed his arm and helped him to his feet, but the weight of him practically crushed her shoulders into dust. "You have that bond. All your thoughts and emotions and secrets pass through it. I thought you would have heard it…"

Bree frowned and thought back to the moment when every barrier between her mind and Taveon's had broken down. She had accepted the bond, fully and completely, and a rush of swirling memories and emotions had torn through her very soul. There had been something…she remembered. Something dark and dangerous Taveon desperately wanted to hide. But it hadn't scared her. Instead, she'd felt more drawn to him than she ever had before.

She had reached out toward him and smiled...

But then the memory had been doused in murky waters, hiding itself from Bree's conscious state. It felt like a distant dream, one she'd had so many years in the past that it had long been lost.

Somewhere deep inside of her, she knew the

answers to all of her questions were there. Hiding and waiting for her to unwrap the truth and see it for its full glory. But right now, it was too far out of her grasp for her to see any part of it at all.

So, for now, she would have to go with what Taveon and Rafe were willing to tell her. Unfortunately, that wasn't much.

❦

Bree and Rafe stumbled through the castle grounds until they reached the Prince's—no, the *King's*—chambers. Taveon had chosen to continue to reside in the rooms he'd had since a small fae boy instead of moving into the rooms of the late King Midas. The two guards standing watch outside in the corridor gave Bree and Rafe a quick glance before immediately opening the doors and ushering them inside.

She hoped that this would work. She didn't know what she would do if it didn't. Rafe had left a trail of blood behind him, and his grip on her arm had weakened with every step they'd made toward Taveon's chambers. She didn't know how much longer he would be able to hold onto consciousness.

"Bree," he wheezed as she lowered him onto Taveon's red satin sofa. "I appreciate what you are attempting to do, but Taveon is in no shape to heal me. If you ask him to try, he may very well end up falling further into his unconsciousness."

"Which is why I don't plan on asking him to try," she chirped, shuffling over to Taveon's tidy desk where she found a pen and ink and a scrap of parchment. "I'm going to ask Taveon what the hell I need to do to fix you, and then I'm going to do it my damn self."

Rafe rubbed a shaky hand down his face. "Bree, I am thankful you are trying to help me, but—oh." Realization dawned in his eyes, and he struggled to sit up higher so that he could watch her every move. "You think that because you're bonded to him, you will be able to use his healing powers."

"Bingo," Bree said, casting a smile over her shoulder as she crossed the room to Taveon's bed. "If he can give me immortality through the bond, then surely he can give me any other power he might have."

But only silence met her ears this time. Rafe pursed his lips, and then shook his head. "I do not like this, Bree. Taveon is in a weakened state, and you have never done this before. What if it somehow harms you? I will not have you—"

But Bree had already begun to block out his argument. She knew there was always a risk attached to trying something new, especially in the Dark Fae realm. But Rafe was injured, so much so that his breathing had become labored. Plus...she was more than a little intrigued to see if she could do it. She'd never enjoyed her ability to transform into a deadly beast, but being able to heal someone? That was the kind of power she truly wished she could wield.

Bree stepped up beside Taveon's bed, and she stared down at his unconscious form. He looked so peaceful like this, like he was far away from all the horror and danger of Underworld. A part of her wished they didn't have to rip that peace away from him. But this was no kind of life to live, not being able to move, not being able to see, not being able to do anything except exist inside your own mind. If it wasn't for Bree, Taveon would have no contact with the outside world. He would not even know if the rest of the realm even existed anymore. And, he would have no one to talk to. He would be trapped inside his own mind forever.

Bree wasn't about to let that happen.

As she stared down at his handsome face, she let every wall between them drop away. In her day-to-day life, Bree forced herself to keep barriers between their minds. It was too much, knowing that Taveon could feel and hear everything that she did. It was the only way to keep some element of herself as hers and hers alone. Wall after wall dropped away, and the very essence of Taveon filled her mind. Strength, power, and a deep kindness that he kept hidden from everyone else. He wanted the Court to think he was hard and cold like his father, but he wasn't. If anything, Taveon was the total opposite of everything King Midas had always been. Probably because Taveon had never really been Midas's son in the first place.

"Bree," Taveon said into her mind, a smile echoing through his words. Bree stared down at his face, slack and still and peaceful. His lips didn't move an inch, but there was no mistaking the lighthearted expression he wanted to show her for her arrival into his mind. Her heart squeezed tight, and a twinge of guilt ran through her. He was probably lonely. He'd spent all these hours alone with nothing to do and no one to talk to. She needed to visit him more often.

"Hi, Taveon." She reached out and placed a soft hand on his arm. His skin was cool to the touch, as if he'd been dunked in a vat of ice. "How's it going in there?"

Bree tried to keep her voice lighthearted, not wanting to scare him, though she knew the terror he would feel when he found out why she was here to see him.

"Oh, you know," Taveon said with a laugh. "I guess you could say I've been doing a lot of thinking. Not much else for me to do. What I would give to have a conversation with anyone, even Lord Dagen."

Bree smiled and squeezed his arm. She wondered if he could feel it, even if he was in this weird, coma-like state. Through their bond, she swore she felt a hand on her skin and the light caress of fingers running up and down her arm. Bree stiffened, her core going tight. What was Taveon doing? Her heart raced, pounding out a frantic beat in her chest.

"What's wrong?" Taveon asked, and the feel of his fingers on her skin fell away. "Something has happened. You did not come here just to say hello, did you? You came here to ask something of me. You came here because something has happened to Rafe."

Taveon could sense exactly what she was feeling through the bond because she'd thrown away all the walls she kept erected between them. Now, there was nothing between them but thoughts and emotions and a million tiny memories that they'd had both together and apart. She could sense his past and his future in this moment right here all at once, and she knew he could sense the same in her. It was almost overwhelming in its intensity, and it was all she could do to not throw up another wall, another barrier, another shield against the onslaught of Taveon in her mind.

"Rafe has been hurt, and we came here to get your help." Even in her mind, Bree's voice trembled.

Sorrow rushed down the bond, and she could practically feel Taveon trying to push through the curse, to force himself out of his coma. He was pounding against invisible walls, trying to get out of his mind and back into the real world.

"I cannot help him, Bree. Not like this. How badly is he hurt?" The pain in his voice matched the pain in her mind when she thought about never being able to see Taveon again, at least not awake and alert and full of life.

"He's bleeding pretty badly," Bree said softly. "And I know you cannot help him, not when you're like...this. But maybe *I* can help him. Or, we can help him. Together. I've used your powers before. Your immortality is running through my veins. Maybe if you instructed me on how to heal him, I could use your power to close his wound."

Taveon fell silent, and it was almost as though he had disappeared behind his own wall. But then he came back, his emotions a whirlwind, so fierce and so tormented that she couldn't pick out a single thought to name. They were blended together, forming a tornado that wanted to suck her up from the ground and draw her into its madness.

"Rafe told you what I can do." Taveon's voice was hard, but she knew it was not directed at Rafe. Even with their bond, and even with the openness between them, Bree knew that Taveon did not want her to know all of the secrets he kept hidden from the world. She knew that she had seen them that day they'd formed the bond between them, but he had still kept them hidden from her ever since.

"I guessed it," she said. "Rafe did not need to tell me in order for me to put the puzzle pieces together. I'm not an idiot, Taveon. He's come to you for healing on more than one occasion. Besides, you've healed me, too."

A pause. "I assumed you thought that it was the making of our bond that healed you." Taveon let out a heavy sigh. "But I should not have assumed anything of the sort. You have shown me time and time again not to underestimate you."

"Glad you're finally figuring it out," Bree said with a smile. "Even if it did take you going into a magical trance to get there. So, can you tell me how to heal Rafe?"

"I worry this will not work, Bree." Taveon's voice was laced with worry. "Perhaps you should go to the Council."

"Does a fae on the Council have special healing powers?"

"No," Taveon admitted. "But Conlan or Dagen might be able to find someone who does."

"We might not have time for that," Bree said with a frown, glancing over to where Rafe had sprawled out on the sofa. Blood had begun to drip down the side of it, dribbling onto the stone floor. Rafe's face, normally golden from the glow reflected from the light of the moon, was now as white as a sheet. His eyes were fixed on her face, but they were distant. They needed to hurry. "He's not in good shape, Taveon. You need to tell me what to do. *Now.*"

"Right." Dread dripped down the bond, pouring into Bree's mind and making her fear ramp up another notch. "Here is what you need to do. Go over, stand by his side, and place your hands directly over his heart. Once you are certain that your hands are where they need to be, close your eyes and tell me that you are ready. I will then send my healing powers through the bond to heal Rafe's body and soul. If we are lucky, this will work, but I have never tried to heal through another fae."

"Well, you've never had this kind of bond with someone before." Bree clutched his arm and squeezed tight. "This is special. This is different. If you're ever going to be able to do something like this, it would be now, and it would be with me."

Bree felt a slight smile travel through the bond. "It is not like you to be the one full of optimism, but I am glad for it. Now, go. Prepare yourself as best you can. I do not know how this is going to feel for you."

Bree gave a nod, and she let go of Taveon's arm, even though she hated breaking the contact between them. Ever since they'd made the bond, she felt the constant desire to be close to him, especially now. She strode across the room and dropped to Rafe's side. Her knees dug into the stone ground, but she ignored the pain. Following Taveon's instructions, she lifted Rafe's shirt to reveal his chest. And then she placed her trembling hands directly over his heart.

His chest was slick and cool underneath her shaking fingers. His heartbeat was rapid but weak at the same time. He groaned and shifted against the sofa. Heart beating wildly in her chest, Bree took in a deep breath and let out a long exhale through her nose.

"Are you certain this is a good idea, Bree?" Rafe asked, his voice just as weak as his heartbeat. He tried to shift up onto his elbows and pry her hands off his chest, but his usual unending strength had left him. Bree had to push her fear aside. It had taken them far too long to get here. It had taken her far too long to talk Taveon into attempting this feat. "I worry what will happen to you when you try to heal me with Taveon's powers. You do not know the truth about him. He is far stronger than you realize. And it is not natural for his abilities to churn through your mortal body."

"I don't care," Bree said, her heart racing. "You look like you're on the edge of death. If this weakens me, then it's worth it."

"I am not worried about it weakening you, Bree." Rafe shuddered as he drew a deep breath into his lungs. "I am worried about it killing you. You do not know how his power will transform your body."

"Well, we're about to find out." Bree took in another deep breath, filling her lungs with the sudden cool of the room. She closed her eyes, and she called out to Taveon through their bond. She'd left all the walls down between them. And he'd been listening to every word of her conversation with Rafe. She knew that he could see his old friend's current state through her eyes, and she could feel his fear pounding deep within his chest.

"I will not let this kill you, Bree," Taveon said, his voice rough with emotion. "Just hold on tight. Let the power fill you. And then let it go. Let it flee your body, even if it feels like every part of your essence is leaving you behind. Let it form in your hands. Let it fill Rafe's soul."

Strange magic took shape in her gut. It started in the very center of her, right within her core. Slowly, it began to spread through her body. Her stomach churned with bright sparks, tingling her lungs and then her chest and then her shoulders. It traveled down her legs, reaching out until it touched the very edges of her toes. And then it filled her head with the sweet, sweet scent of the morning after rain. Bree shattered against the sensation, her entire body trembling from the intensity of its fire. She felt alive. She'd never felt this alive in her entire life. Every part of her was full of him, full of Taveon.

And she didn't want to let it go. She wanted to reach out and hold it close to her, forever trapping his essence inside her form.

Rafe moaned, snapping Bree back into the present. Another deep breath. Another long exhale through her nose. The sparkling filled her head, lighting up the back of her eyelids with visions of a bright sun that filled the world with the sweetest kind of light. For a moment, she hesitated, curious about that bright light. There was no sun in Underworld. Only a moon and the darkest of nights. And yet...

"Let the healing go, Bree," Taveon whispered into her mind.

Shuddering, Bree focused on Rafe's uneven heartbeat. She focused on her hands, on her fingertips, and on pushing every part of her out through the very edges of her skin. The magical, sparkling rays of light pooled into her hands, and her head felt light from the sudden absence of it. Her arms crackled and shook, and the magic poured out of her body and into Rafe. He began to shake underneath her, his body now feeling the same sensation she had.

He was healing, taking the magic from both Bree and Taveon. His skin began to warm, and his heartbeat grew stronger. So strong that she could feel the force of it pounding through his skin as she pressed her hands as tightly to his chest as she could.

"You did it, Bree," Taveon whispered into her mind, and then the sensation snapped away as he pulled himself away from her.

Shaking her head, Bree opened her eyes to find Rafe gazing up at her with eyes full of an emotion that she was far too scared to name. His hand reached up to her face, and he trailed a finger down her cheek, stopping to catch the tear that had fallen from her eyes. She was crying. But she hadn't realized it until now.

She didn't even know why she was crying. Nothing was wrong. Quite the opposite in fact. She had used Taveon's power, and Rafe had been healed. His wound had begun to stitch itself together, and he was no longer bleeding.

And Bree was fine. Taveon's power hadn't killed her. It hadn't even harmed her. She just felt... impossibly empty now, as if she had just lost a very important part of her.

CHAPTER 8
TAVEON

Taveon felt weaker due to the amount of strength that Bree had pulled from his body, but he did not mind. He would do it again a million times, just as long as Rafe survived. And he had. Against all odds, Bree had managed to heal Rafe by using Taveon's healing powers.

But Taveon had felt Bree's desire to hold onto that power. He had felt her drawn to that bright, sparkling light that he saw every time he healed a fae. And she had wondered at it, knowing that no part of Underworld ever saw light quite like that. There was no sun there. There was nothing more than a full moon sky lit up by sparkling stars.

He had managed to draw her away from that realization, but he knew it was only a matter of time before her mind drifted back to it, wondering at what it meant. She had come so close so many times to understanding the full truth of him, but he never wanted her to get that close ever again. It would be dangerous for her to know the truth. Not for Taveon but for Bree.

Taveon reached out through the bond and caressed Bree's mind with his own. She was there in an instant, her heart open wide to let him into her soul. Everything within him ached from a kind of desire he had long since felt. He wished he could do more than speak to her in his own mind. He wished he could wrap his arms around her and hold her close.

"Is something wrong?" she asked.

"No," he said. "Nothing more than the usual. I wanted to ask something of you, Bree, though I hate to do so."

"What is it?" she asked. "I'll do anything you need me to do, you know."

"Just as long as you promise that you will keep yourself safe. Do not be reckless. No matter what."

"I promise," she said, though Taveon knew deep down inside that this was not a promise Bree could keep. She was reckless and determined and brave. Once she set her mind to a task, to hell with all the rest. He just hoped she understood how careful he wanted her to be. Her safety was far more important to him than anything else. But he also knew she needed something to do or she would drive herself and everyone around her crazy.

"I need you to look into the curse for me. Quietly. Listen and watch. Learn what you can." A pause. "My father had old tomes in his chambers. Perhaps you might find some answers there, or perhaps you might be able to overhear someone in the Court discussing what has happened."

"Is that it?" He could feel her smile through the bond. "I was going to do that anyway, you know. You didn't need to ask."

"Thank you, Bree," he said, hating that she had to be the one to protect him instead of the other way around. He wanted to be her savior. He wanted to be strong and powerful. For her.

"No problem. Leave it with me. I'll find whoever did this to you. And I'll make them bring you back to me."

CHAPTER 9
BREE

Fillan hadn't shown his face since he'd snuck into Bree's quarters, but she felt his presence hovering around her like a clingy fog no matter how hard she tried to forget what he'd asked her to do. Truth be told, she was more than a little curious to find the answer to his question. What was Taveon's secret?

The answer to that question might very well lead to the more important one: who had put Taveon under his curse? And how could they fix it?

So far, the council had managed to keep the truth about the King's current state held tight within the castle walls, but it was only a matter of time before the news began to spread throughout the Dark Fae lands. One little spark was all it would take for the entire Court to go up in flames, leaving behind nothing more than the ashy remains of everyone inside.

The only way to stop it would be to find out the answer to Bree's questions before enemies discovered Taveon's fate.

Bree took a deep breath as she stared out her window at the setting moon. Soon, full darkness would consume the skies, and every fae in the castle would turn to their beds for sleep. It was the perfect time to snoop around. She needed to find some answers.

Bree waited a few more hours and then doused the light in her room, along with the flickering fire that kept her quarters warm from the cold that had begun to seep into the castle as the nights grew colder. Underworld did not have fully distinguishable seasons like the human and Light Fae realms. Instead, they had two "stages" of the year. Cold and Warm. Now, the Cold was slowly creeping in, and Bree couldn't help but wonder what this nighttime place would look like in the snow.

As she poked her head out the door, she let out a slow exhale of relief when she saw the corridor was dark, empty, and as silent as the deepest part of a forest. She did not take any light with her, choosing her own eyes instead of a candle's bright flame. Rafe had taught her how to shift single body parts when needed, and her beastly eyes could see in the dark far better than her 'human' eyes could see in the light.

The floorboards creaked underneath as she slowly shut her door behind her. Taking in a deep breath, she focused on the path ahead and made her way down the deathly-silent hallways of the castle. Tonight, she would hunt for answers.

B ree stepped inside the former King's chambers. In his absence, the room felt like a tomb, and the echo of his presence resounded through the lofted stone space like a dying heartbeat. Shivering, she hugged her arms to her chest and shifted her eyes back to normal after spotting a candle on the table just inside the door.

After lighting the flame, Bree held the candle aloft before her and gazed from one end of the room to the other. If someone had asked her how she imagined King Midas's private chambers to be, this was pretty close to what she would have described.

Along the far wall hung skulls of varying shapes and sizes. Some looked human—or fae. Others looked beastly, their sharp edges glinting against the candlelight. There were probably a hundred of them, and Bree had no desire to know where they'd come from, how, or why. Victims, she imagined. Fae and beasts who had fallen against the King's sword. Some of them had likely been enemies, though she knew Midas had often been a fan of putting heads on stakes just outside the front gates as a reminder to the realm of his unyielding strength.

To her left was a bed, but it was unlike any bed she'd ever seen. There were no sheets. No pillows. Just a slab of stone erected high above the floor. Midas wasn't the kind of fae who valued comfort, a fact that was reflected even in his most private of spaces.

More than ever, she was glad she'd never had to meet the male.

A click resounded in the heavy silence, and Bree whirled toward the door. Dagen stood just inside, his eyes widening when he spotted her skulking around in the midst of the previous King's quarters. Bree's heart began to race. Not out of fear but from something else. Something she couldn't quite name.

"Bree?" Dagen lifted his eyebrows, and then quickly closed the door behind him. "What in the name of the forest are you doing in here? If one of the guards caught you, they would—"

"They'd what?" she asked, propping her free hand on her waist. "Throw me in the dungeons? Been there. Done that. Besides, I'm acting under Taveon's orders."

"You honestly expect me to believe that the King commanded you to lurk around in his father's chambers?"

Bree's heart lurched at that. As much as she kept trying to tell herself that she was doing this for

Taveon, deep down she knew that part of it was because she was dying to know what he was hiding. But she wasn't about to tell Lord Dagen that.

"He asked me to look into who might have cast this curse or whatever it is, so yes." Bree crossed the room, daring to draw closer to Dagen's side. "But what I really want to know is why are *you* here, Lord Dagen?"

His eyes glinted as he watched her take one slow step after the other. "I may not have a direct line to the King's mind, but I know what he wishes all the same. I, too, am here to find answers."

"Oh?" Bree paused, halfway between the back wall of skulls and where Dagen still stood beside the iron door. She couldn't help but notice how he looked against the flickering candlelight. The shadows curled around his sharp features, and there was something in the way he threw his shoulders back that made him look far more powerful than he usually did. Strength shimmered around his thick frame, radiating straight into Bree's core.

Bree had always thought Dagen to be handsome, but it was a fact she'd desperately tried to ignore. But now, they were alone. Just the two of them. And no one at all knew they were here. Not even Taveon. She'd erected too many walls around her mind before heading out on her mission for him to follow her here.

Her heart beat a little faster.

"I know you may find it hard to believe, but I too care about what happens to our ruler."

"You care what happens to the *King*," Bree said, blinking out of her reverie. "But you do not care what happens to Taveon himself. You just care about the position, not about the male occupying it."

Dagen pursed his lips. "That is not fair, Bree. After everything that has happened, you still think I am some kind of heartless monster?"

"Honestly?" Bree lifted her hands to her sides and shrugged. "I don't really know what to think about you. One minute, you seem like you're working against Taveon. The next, you're working with him and then for him. I have no idea what it is you want. Or why you want it. And what you'd do in order to get it."

The words fell out of her mouth in a rush. They were thoughts that had been building inside of her since she'd come to Underworld, to this castle, to this strange world where the truth of fae could not be taken at face value. Yes, Dagen had "redeemed" himself by finally taking Taveon's side during the Battle for the Crown, but why had he done it? And was it all just some sort of act? He had been the one who had asked Bree to spy for him in the first place. He'd been the one who had almost turned Bree against Taveon completely.

No matter what he'd done since then, those were facts that she could never, ever forget.

"What I want is what I have always wanted: what is best for this realm. For the longest time, I did not believe that Taveon was that, but I have now seen the error in my ways." He took a step closer, and Bree's body went tense. "What is best for this realm is for our King, who was crowned only days ago, to take command. We need him on his throne. Not in his bed. I shudder to think what will happen if we cannot save him."

So, he had come to the very same conclusion Bree had. Not a surprise considering that he was an expert on all things political, and he'd been the Hand of the King for Midas. Hell, he was probably three steps ahead of Bree already.

She gave him a slight nod and decided to give him the benefit of the doubt for once. "Have you found anything?"

Lifting his eyebrows, he crossed his arms over his chest. "Have *you* found anything, Bree?"

"No." A beat passed. "But maybe we'd be better off combining forces."

She couldn't believe she was suggesting it. Only days before, she'd sworn to herself to never work with Dagen again, but here she was. Asking and hoping and praying he'd say yes. Searching for answers alone made no sense. Together, they could cover far more ground and much more quickly. Taveon would be back on his feet a hell of a lot faster if Bree swallowed her pride.

It was a long while before Dagen deemed to answer, loosing a breath as he ran a hand down his face. "You will have to excuse my surprise, Bree. It was not very long ago that you were insistent on staying away from me."

"Yeah, well. I think maybe I made a mistake, too, and now I'm seeing the error of my ways. We're better off working together on this. I want what's best for the realm, too, and what's best is getting this curse off of Taveon as quickly as possible."

"Good. Then, it is settled. We will work together on this."

"Okay," Bree said with a nod. "What did you have in mind?"

Dagen stepped closer to her, and Bree swore she could feel his masculine power radiating off his body in waves. "We need to get the entire Court in one room again. Look each fae in the eye. See if we can prod them for information. Someone must know something."

"All in one room," Bree repeated. She was following the conversation but only slightly. Somehow, she'd gotten a little preoccupied with his lips. They were so very close to hers, and she felt inexplicably drawn to them. She licked her own lips, wondering if he could feel the same tension she did.

"We had the celebration after the coronation, but it is not unheard of for a new King to throw a separate ball not long after he takes the throne. It is a way to..." Dagen stopped speaking when Bree licked her lips again. "Bree."

"Yes?" she asked, body buzzing from electricity.

"You are distracting me."

"No, you're the one distracting me," she whispered.

He reached up and cupped her cheek with his palm, sighing as she leaned against his touch. She couldn't help herself. There was something about Lord Dagen that called to her. Whatever bond they shared, it was far different than what she shared with Taveon and with Rafe, but there was no denying that it was there. At times, she'd been able to push it aside but not now. She wanted comfort and closeness. And she wanted it from him.

"Bree," he whispered softly. "What has changed in you? I thought you..."

He left off his final words, but Bree knew what they were all the same. He thought she hated him. And she had. Well, kind of. She had distrusted him. She had feared his motivations were not what they had seemed. And, truth be told, she still couldn't be certain that he was being genuine.

It didn't change the fact that she wanted nothing more than to feel his lips on her skin.

"Kiss me," she said, finding a courage she did not know she had. "Please."

He sucked in a ragged breath and drew her closer, drinking her in with his bright eyes. He pulled her mouth toward his and kissed her hard, his fingers digging into the strands of her hair. She moaned against him, letting herself get lost in the feel of him. He held her with a strength and certainty that made her knees shake.

Bree pressed her body against him, her breasts brushing against his chest. The moan that escaped his throat sent a tight thrill through her gut. Her fingers fumbled with his tunic, a new intense desire sweeping through her core. She no longer just wanted to kiss him. She wanted to feel him. Every part of him. And she wanted him inside of her now.

Her fingers dipped into his waistband, and he gasped. Suddenly, he was five feet across the room, his hair disheveled and his cheeks pink. Disappointment churned in her gut, as well as embarrassment. Did he not want her, too?

"Not like this, Bree. Not here." He gazed around them at the skulls and the bones. King Midas's chambers. She had to admit that it wasn't the sexiest place she could think of, but that hadn't seemed to matter five seconds ago.

"You're just trying to turn me down gently," she said, twisting away so that he could not see the hurt on her face.

"I am not turning you down," he said, voice insistent. "But I cannot be with you the way I want to. Not like this. Come back to my quarters with me. Let us leave Midas's rooms behind. His ghost haunts this place."

But Bree shook her head. The moment had passed, and now she felt like a massive idiot for throwing herself at Dagen in the first place. She'd had a moment of weakness, one she couldn't have again.

Dagen blinked and gave a nod. "Very well, Bree. If that is what you wish. Then, I suppose I will see you tomorrow. Come to my office when you're done with training. We will work out the details for our ball. And we'll find whoever has done this to the King."

CHAPTER 10

BREE

In the mornings, Bree trained with Rafe, Eurig, and Lyra. Before, she had always looked forward to her time with Rafferty, but Eurig was making the Academy practically unbearable these days.

Rafe clapped his hands and raised his voice when his three trainees had joined him in the center of the room. Eurig had been late. As always. "Today, we're going to be working on building your strength."

Bree smiled. This was one exercise she was used to. They had worked on it together before the new recruits had arrived. Bree would shift into her beast, and she would pick up pieces of stone off the floor until she was too weary to continue. She flexed her hands and smiled when her claws immediately responded to her call.

"Not like that today, Bree," Rafe said before Bree could get too far into her shift.

Frowning, Bree let her claws snap back into her skin. "Then, like how?"

"In your fae forms," he said with a tight smile, knowing how she'd feel about this particular brand of training. "There will be times when you are unable to fight in your beastly form, where staying fae is a far better option. And we need to train your abilities as a fae, just as much as we need to train your beast."

With a sigh, Bree nodded. She knew he was right, but that didn't mean she had to like it. The truth was, Bree's fae form was far weaker than her beast. And no matter how much training she did, she doubted she would ever excel without her wolf.

Eurig, on the other hand, looked smug as hell.

"What are you smiling at?" she snapped.

He lifted his shoulder in a shrug. "With those puny arms of yours, I should have guessed you wouldn't be happy about training your strength. I bet you cannot even do a single push-up."

She glared at him. "Excuse me? Did you just call my arms *puny*?"

"Prove to me they aren't then," he said with a smile, and crossed his arms over his chest.

Bree stomped over to him, sizing him up. Okay, so he was massive, but she wasn't going to let that stop her from showing him up. Not that she could really show him up. He had muscles larger than her head, and it didn't look like he even had an ounce of body fat. If she tried to punch him, she'd probably hurt herself far worse than she'd hurt him. But she could not *stand* the smug expression on his face.

He didn't expect her to actually do anything. She could tell by the glint in his eye. He knew that she knew just how much of a muscular tank he was. Sometimes, the element of surprise was everything.

So, Bree pulled back her fist and slammed it straight into Eurig's stomach. Pain lanced through her hand as a crunch echoed through the room. She cried out loud, doubling over at the sharp stabs that shot through her knuckles.

Shit!

Tears sprung into her eyes, but she blinked them away. She couldn't bear the thought of him seeing her crying after she'd just tried to punch him in the chest. Out of the corner of her eye, she could see that he hadn't budged an inch from her attack. He just stood there looking at her as if nothing had happened at all.

"Bree." Rafe's soft hand was on her back. "Are you okay?"

"I'm fine," she said through gritted teeth. And, in fact, she *was* fine. The pain in her hand had already begun to ebb away. Taveon's healing powers poured through her veins and pooled around her throbbing knuckles, softening them until the bones clicked back into place.

Rafferty stared at her hand, frowning. "Do you need to—?"

"No," she said firmly. She would not let Eurig get the better of her. "I'm fine. Let's continue with training."

Rafe gave a nod but leaned down to whisper in her ear before he left. "Try not to punch your fellow trainees, eh?"

Heat filled her cheeks, and she kept her gaze focused on Rafe. She knew that Eurig was still staring at her, but she wouldn't give him the satisfaction of letting him look into her eyes. Instead, she pretended he wasn't there for the rest of the session.

Rafe had them doing all sorts of bone-wearying tasks. They ran sprints from one side of the domed room to the other. He counted out push-ups. First, they did ten. Then, they did twenty. Somewhere, he'd found a rope that he hung from the ceiling, and they were forced to climb to the top at least once.

Bree could only make it halfway up before her limbs gave out. When she fell hard onto the stone floor, she could have sworn she heard Eurig laugh.

At the end of the session, Bree could barely think straight. She stumbled down the corridor back to her quarters, but a hulking monstrosity stepped right into her path to block her way.

"You look as though you've been trampled by horses," Eurig said.

She stopped short and glared at him. "Get out of

my way, Eurig. I really don't feel like fighting you right now."

He lifted an eyebrow. "Funny, *you* were the one who punched *me*. You never even gave me the chance to fight back."

"Is that why you're here?" she barked out a laugh, though she could barely manage the words with the weariness that clung to her bones. Her knees almost buckled, and she had to place a hand on the wall just to keep herself upright. "Fine. Hit me then."

But instead of knocking her flat onto her ass, Eurig swept Bree off the ground and into his arms. Irritation flickered through her, and she hated how she could feel his muscles ripple as he held her close to his chest.

"Put me down," she said through gritted teeth. "Where are you taking me?"

"To your room." He kicked open the door to her quarters and dumped her unceremoniously on her bed. "You looked liked you were going to pass out. Get some rest, Bree. You'll need to be ready for round two tomorrow."

CHAPTER 11

BREE

O ver the next week, ball preparations combined with the new Academy training schedule meant that Bree barely had time to eat, let alone seek Rafferty out for the kind of intimacy she yearned to share with him. It turned out that a courtly ball, hosting most of the prominent members of Dark Fae society, took a lot more work than Bree had given Dagen credit for.

There was the menu to sort out, the various ingredients needed to cook each course. The wine and the spirits. The musicians, the tables, the decorations. She and Dagen were in charge of it all, and while it was a 'fake' ball in a way, both of them wanted to get it right.

It would be the first ball since Taveon's coronation, and many of the fae would be expecting something grand from their new King. Most of them had no idea that he would not be in attendance.

Bree strode through Dagen's open door after another brutal training session and plopped onto his sofa. He sat behind his dark wooden desk, frowning down at a long stretch of parchment that she knew held the list of all the names who would be attending the next day's celebration.

"While I enjoy your company at every turn, Bree, might you not choose to change out of your training leathers before our planning sessions? Surely you would be more comfortable in...something else."

Bree snorted and shot him a grin. "Trust me. I'm far more comfortable in these clothes than I would be if I wore some stuffy dress."

The truth was, Bree had kept her fighting leathers from the Light Fae realm. Rafferty had given her a few Dark Fae sets, but she kept on going back to the ones she'd worn on that fateful day when she'd left her old realm behind. Something about them...comforted her. It felt like an anchor to the past, to who she had used to be. Sometimes, like now when everything was so up in the air, she needed that reminder.

Lord Dagen's gaze flicked up and down her torso. "They do suit you, I admit. Though you look particularly stunning in gowns."

Her cheeks flushed, which was ridiculous. One little compliment and she'd turned ten shades redder. Things had been strangely tense and electric between them since that day in King Midas's chambers. Neither of them had brought up the kiss...and Bree had no intention of doing so now either. If Dagen wanted to pretend like it had never happened, then Bree would, too.

"How is your training going?" Dagen asked, breaking the tense silence between them.

"Honestly?" Bree let out a belabored sigh. "I liked it a lot better when Eurig wasn't around to scowl and throw his whole alpha-ness into everything we do. Did you know that Rafe has us working on our strength now? In our fae forms, not in our shapeshifter bodies. Push-ups, pull-ups, sprints, the works. And every single damn time, Eurig shows me up."

"A better physical demonstration of power does not mean that Eurig is stronger than you."

"Yeah?" Bree frowned, not convinced. "So, then what does it mean?"

Dagen placed the parchment on his desk, stood, and strode over to the sofa. "It merely means that he has built more muscle than you have. He is larger. But not necessarily better. He is certainly not faster."

"Hmm. He took Rafe down in a fight."

"You have gone head to head with our King Taveon, who I daresay is much more impressive than some outposter who has lived on wooden docks in the middle of the sea his entire life."

Dagen was right. Kind of. But there was something about Eurig that kept getting under Bree's skin. She wanted to beat him, somehow, even though they were not competing in anything. And she wanted him to see just how powerful she could be, if only to see the look of respect on his face.

One day. One day, she would be the one to win.

☙❧

Training had been called off the next morning in preparation for the night's upcoming celebration. So, instead of beating up her body in a million different ways, Bree took a luxurious bath and styled her hair in long loose waves around her shoulders. She donned a new gown to celebrate the occasion. It was silver blue and flowed softly down her body, hugging her waist and her hips. The sleeves opened wide at the ends, revealing her long and slender arms.

This time, she attended the ball alone. She and Dagen had decided to split up and roam through the crowd on their own, each listening for curious conversations. When Bree stepped through the large double doors, the crowd that had gathered took her breath away. It seemed there were more fae in attendance than there had been at the Silver Moon Ball, and the expansive space was practically heaving with evening revellers.

Bree dropped back her head and gazed up at the

ceiling. It had been decorated with a million tiny glowing balls of light. This had been Dagen's doing, Bree thought as her stomach clenched tight. She scanned the crowd, seeking out his familiar face. Everything within her wanted to speak to him, to look into his eyes once again. She had been wrong not to follow him back to his quarters that night, and she wanted nothing more than to see that warmth in his face once again.

But instead, Eurig stepped in front of her, still wearing his golden fighting leathers. Just like always. He was so large that he blocked out everything behind him, forcing Bree to drink him in. He had given his hair another cut, not that it had needed it. But Bree couldn't help but notice that his groom had only highlighted the strong lines of his jaw and his neck.

Bree stepped back, hating the way her face flushed with heat. "I'm surprised you bothered to come tonight. You didn't seem particularly interested in the ball before."

"That's because we were at training. Silly matters like balls are not important when *you* are learning how to fight."

Bree rolled her eyes. She didn't miss the way he'd phrased his sentence, pointedly directed right at her. In his mind, he wasn't the one learning how to fight, because he already knew how. Bree, on the other hand, needed all the help she could get.

And she hated that he was right.

Not that she would admit that to his face.

"Whatever. I have important business to attend to," she said dismissively and stepped to the side to move around his hulking frame. "Enjoy the party. Or don't."

"I heard this was your idea." Eurig let out a snort and shook his head. "I should have known. Only a human would decide something so trivial would be the answer to the King's current state."

Bree tensed. "What the hell do you know about the King's current state?"

He hadn't been at the aftermath of the coronation. Bree was certain of it. There had only been a handful of fae left, and she would have remembered his face —and his body—if he'd been amongst them. If word was beginning to spread...it was only a matter of time before the entire Court found out.

Eurig leaned closer, dropping his voice into a low growl. "I know that the King will not be attending tonight's ball, despite it being a celebration of his new reign. Whatever curse has befallen him, a para-lyzed fae cannot walk, let alone dine and dance to music all night."

"How did you find out?" Bree snapped. "Who told you?"

If there was a leak, Bree needed to find it quickly. And plug it.

Eurig let out a low chuckle, and the scent of mint,

cinnamon, and sea filled her nose. "Relax. Rafferty informed me of the King's condition when I first joined the Academy. And there is no need to worry about me. I will not reveal your precious Taveon's condition to anyone else."

Irritation bubbled up from deep within her gut. "Well, there's no need to be an ass about it."

"You are right. There's no need." He winked. "But it's certainly more fun to be. I not only know about your precious male's curse, but I know about your bond. And your feelings for him are written all across that cute little pixie face of yours."

Bree ground her teeth together and fought the urge to show Eurig exactly how far her training had come in the past few weeks. "Don't call me cute."

"And why is that, Bree? Because you're a vicious beast and not a sweet little thing with a tiny nose?" And then he tapped her nose with his forefinger. He actually bopped her nose. Bree was so taken aback that she didn't have the chance to react until he'd already strode away from her, disappearing into the heaving crowd. She blinked after him, stunned.

She couldn't believe he'd just bopped her nose, like she was a cute little pet.

Fisting her hands, she began to stride after him but another male fae slid into her way before she had the chance. He was tall and lithe, his face hidden by a mask. But Bree would recognize his aura no matter what he did to try to obscure his identity.

She narrowed her eyes and stepped back. "Why are you here?"

Bree didn't say Fillan's name, even though a part of her knew she probably should. He was infamous, but most of the fae in this room had never actually laid eyes on him before. When Fillan had first shown up in her life, Taveon and Dagen had both given her a grim warning: Fillan never lets a fae see him unless he plans on assassinating them. Or unless he wants something.

Still, if she spoke his name aloud, every fae in the room would know exactly who he was.

"I need to speak to you," he said quietly as he wrapped a tight grip around her arm. "Alone. And I would appreciate it if you did not make a scene."

"You're asking *me* to not make a scene? You're the one who showed up here in the middle of a ball meant to celebrate our Court. Not to mention the host of other things you've done." Like kissing her in front of Branok and Conlan, for one.

"Meet me on the other side of the tapestry," he said in an urgent tone, ignoring every other statement she'd made. "And do so quickly."

Fillan drifted away from her, letting his body fall into the churn of the crowd. She watched his back slowly melt from her view, anger and fear roiling through her. Logically, Bree knew what she should do. Go straight to Dagen or Rafe and tell them what had just happened. But the logical part of her brain was drowned out by curiosity. Had Fillan found something? He knew about Taveon's curse. Perhaps he'd somehow found out how to break it.

Or he'd discovered what the color of Taveon's wings meant.

So, with a deep breath, she followed him through the crowd. She slowed to a stop by the fluttering tapestry. It was the same one that had hung there during the last ball. It was a deep crimson red, and a large pair of wings had been sown into the fabric. King Midas's symbol, one intended to remind his subjects of his power and strength.

Red wings meant raw power. The kind that could not be contested or matched. Most Dark Fae had black wings.

And Taveon had silver ones, a trait so rare that she had been forbidden to speak of it, even with Lord Dagen.

Oh, how badly she wanted to know what that meant.

Bree dipped beneath the tapestry and ran face first into Fillan's chest. Cheeks flaming, she took a step back and smoothed down the front of her dress, as if she'd somehow wrinkled it, even though she'd done nothing of the sort. She just needed something to do with her hands. Something that did not involve reaching out and touching Fillan. Anywhere.

He is an assassin, Bree.

So, why did he look like nothing of the sort? Sure,

he came across as deadly and as dangerous as any of the Dark Fae, but he did not hold that darkness as heavily on his shoulders as the rest. There was something lighthearted in his eyes. Something softer and kinder than most of the fae she'd met so far. And yet, he was a killer.

Perhaps his smile was merely a mask, just like Taveon's mask of brutality and Dagen's mask of indifference. Because Taveon was as far from brutal as one could get, and Dagen cared far more than he wanted anyone to know.

Fillan cracked a grin, crinkling the corners of his eyes. "You look flustered."

"Yes, well." She swallowed hard. "You caught me off guard. You know, just like you usually do. Are you even capable of showing up like a normal person instead of some kind of creepy wraith?"

He pressed a hand to his heart and mimed stumbling back. "Ouch. A wraith? How positively horrid."

Bree crossed her arms over her chest. "Don't pretend to be offended. You're anything but. Anyway, get on with it. Why the big cloak and dagger scene? What's so urgent that you had to show yourself in the middle of the party?"

"I did not show myself. Fillan lifted his mask over his head to reveal his very chiseled jaw. "Now, I am showing myself. To you and you alone."

Something about the way he spoke those words made Bree's heart rage like a bull let loose in a crowd.

"I've come to warn you that—" He stopped suddenly and cocked his head. A strange expression crossed his face, one that was something akin to half-irritation and half-amusement. "Oh, here we go again."

Fillan's arm shot out, and he wrapped it around Bree's waist before she had any idea what was happening. She let out a sharp cry of alarm, but his mouth landed on her lips before any sound could escape between them. Eyes wide, she wrapped her hands around his arms and half-heartedly tried to push him away. But then she felt the tightly-coiled biceps and felt the hardness of his perfectly-formed chest. And his lips…they shot a delicious thrill down to her toes, and her entire body sighed against him.

Traitor, Bree thought to herself. Her treacherous body would just not listen to the warnings she screamed inside her head. *He's dangerous. Get away from him. Run! Run very far away...*

But instead, she curled toward him, her back arching as his soft lips moved sensually against hers…

"Not again," a sharp voice called out from behind her.

With a gasp, Bree jumped back at least five feet to put as much distance between her and Fillan as she could. Her heart lurched against her ribs, rattling like the tracks of a train. She spun on her feet, knowing exactly what she would find before she even saw it.

Conlan and Branok. Again. And they were scowling at her as if she were the grossest bug they'd ever laid eyes on.

"Lord Conlan. Lord Branok." She gave each a slight bow of her head. "I can explain."

"No need to," Conlan said as he narrowed his eyes. "Clearly, your affection for the King only goes so far. If you want to lie in bed with an assassin, it's your head, not ours."

CHAPTER 12

BREE

Bree whirled on Fillan, her heart racing. She pushed him once. Then twice. "What the hell was that all about? How dare you fake kiss me again! You knew they were coming, didn't you? What's the point of this? Are you trying to turn the Court against me?"

"Relax." He gave Bree a lopsided grin, leaned against the wall, and crossed his arms over his muscular chest. "No need to be angry about the falseness of it. If you would like a *real* kiss now, I am more than happy to oblige."

Bree's mouth dropped open. "You can't be serious."

His gaze turned dark, dangerous, and thrilling. Bree shivered as he closed the space between them. "More than serious. Just admit you want a kiss from me, and I will show you the difference in one that is all for show and one that is very much real."

Blinking, Bree shook her head, hating how hot her cheeks suddenly felt. "Stop messing with me."

"Very well." Fillan stepped back, sucking all the warmth of his body away along with him. She yearned to pull him back. Because a part of her truly was curious about that kiss. If that toe-curling one had only been fake, she couldn't imagine how it would feel if he put his emotions into it…

"I came here to warn you that I have heard an attack is planned for tonight. I do not know what and I do not know when. Or by who." His gaze locked on Bree's. "Just know that there will likely be death this night."

Bree shivered, eyes going as wide as the moon. All the heat she'd felt moments before drained from her face. "An attack? Where did you hear that?"

"I cannot reveal my sources. Not even to you." He stepped closer once again and dropped the ghost of a kiss on her forehead. The touch made her eyes flutter shut, and she leaned toward him, body yearning for more even in the midst of the terrible information he'd just provided to her. "Be careful, Bree."

A cool burst of mist swarmed over Bree's skin, and she opened her eyes to find nothing but blank space before her. Fillan had vanished. Again. But not before telling her that someone had planned an attack on the Court this night. She needed to find

Dagen before it was too late. He could alert the guards and clear the Great Hall without making too much of a scene. Panic was the last thing they needed, and if the Court got wind of an impending attack, they would question Taveon's ability to protect them from harm.

Bree ducked under the tapestry. Conlan and Branok were already waiting for her. Their faces were twin scowls as they took in her wide eyes, her flushed cheeks, and her lips that still ached for more of Fillan's touch.

"I assume you are somehow keeping your dalliances with the assassin hidden from Taveon, even with your bond," Conlan said, pursing his lips. "But be assured, Redcap girl, we will inform him once he returns to the world of the living. We let it go once. We will not let it go again. You are clearly involved with Fillan, and the King needs to know exactly what one of his closest advisors is involved with."

Bree didn't want to imagine the look on Taveon's face when he found out she'd been caught kissing Fillan—twice. But she couldn't also help the thrill that went through her at Conlan's words. Taveon considered her one of his closest advisors. It was a thought that warmed her far more than she would have expected.

"Honestly, it's not what it looked like." Or was it? "And there are more important things to worry about right now. Fillan told me that there will be an attack on the Court tonight. We need to tell the guards so they can calmly and quickly clear the hall."

Branok's eyebrows lifted to the top of his forehead. "And did he warn you of this alleged attack before or after he took you to his bed?"

Her neck filled with an impossible heat. "He didn't take me to bed. It was just a kiss. One that I didn't ask for, by the way."

But it had definitely been one she'd enjoyed...

"You are new here, Bree," Conlan said softly, though not gently. "So, you will not be as aware of Fillan's reputation as you should be. This would not be the first time he lied in order to get a female to do his bidding."

Bree gaped at the Lord. "What are you talking about? Lord Dagen said that Fillan never revealed himself to anyone he did not intend to kill."

"Dagen may have...exaggerated. Most likely in hope of getting you to stay away from Fillan." Branok and Conlan exchanged a weighted glance. "Fillan may have a reputation as an accomplished assassin, but he also has a reputation with the females. He is... quite popular, it seems, and he is able to charm his way into anyone's bed."

"Females," Conlan said with a bark. "Why they are attracted to an assassin is beyond me."

Irritation flickered through Bree. Strangely, she felt kind of...jealous. Even though their kiss had been all for show, the way he kept showing up as some kind of wraith-like savior had made Bree feel a little special. But clearly that wasn't the case if he was making girls around the realm swoon at any chance he got.

"Look." She cleared her throat. "There was no taking to bed, okay? Fillan was being serious. There's an attack planned on the Court tonight."

Branok and Conlan exchanged skeptical glances once again. "I doubt he was being as honest as you thought he was. Even if he is right, ending the ball early would do far more harm than good."

Conlan gave a nod, continuing. "It would only signal to the rest of the realm that something is wrong here."

"There are guards stationed all around the castle grounds. Experienced males who are far more powerful than a random attacker," Branok said. "No weapons are allowed in, and no one can get in or out without being vetted first."

"Fillan got in, didn't he?" Bree pointed out.

Conlan waved his hand dismissively. "Fillan is a unique case. If he wanted to carry out an attack on the Court, putting an end to the ball would not stop him in the least."

Shaking her head, Bree took two steps back away from the Lords. "So, you're going to do nothing."

Smiling, Conlan grabbed a glass of wine from a passing servant before crossing the space to press it into Bree's hands. "No, I am going to enjoy myself. And you should, too."

"Do what you came here to do, Bree. Mingle. Make sure everyone thinks the King is fine. And keep an ear out for anything that might point toward whoever is behind his curse."

Bree curled her fingers tight around the wine glass and tipped back her head to empty the contents into her mouth. The bitter liquid burned her throat as it slid into her stomach, but it didn't stop her from grabbing another and drinking it just as fast. When she was done, she wiped her sleeve against her lips and stormed away from the Lords who still watched over the proceedings in the corner with their nonchalant expressions pasted across their faces.

They might not care about Fillan's warnings but Dagen would. She needed to find him. Quickly before—

A massive body stepped in front of her. She glanced up. Eurig.

With a frustrated sigh, she pressed against his chest, but he didn't budge even the slightest. "What are you doing, Eurig? Can you please get out of my way?"

"Somehow, you get even ruder when you drink." He lifted his chin, eyes glittering. "Where are you off to in such a hurry? I saw you sneaking behind the tapestry and then back, and those Lords over there did not look particularly happy to see you."

"None of your damn business," Bree snapped before letting out a heavy sigh and pushing at his chest. "Move. It's important, Eurig."

His eyes flicked across her face, and he frowned. "Something is wrong."

"Yeah, no shit."

"Tell me, Bree," he said in a low voice.

"Why would I tell you of all people?" she asked. "You've done nothing but convince me that you'd rather see this Court burn down than anything else."

"That is not true." Eurig's gaze went razor sharp, and he nodded, as if he suddenly understood every thought whirring through Bree's mind. "Is someone in danger?"

Bree sighed. As much as she hated to fill Eurig in on what was happening, she knew he wasn't going to leave her be unless she spilled. "*Everyone* is in danger. There have been reports of an attack planned for tonight. I need to find Dagen or Rafe and tell them what's happening so they can get everyone out of here safely."

Eurig gave a nod, and suddenly he was all business. "You take that half of the Great Hall. I will take this one. We will find the others more quickly if we split up. What should I tell them if I find them first? Who is attacking?"

Bree shook her head. "I don't know. I don't know anything but what I've told you."

Eurig regarded her carefully, his expression full of

wariness. "Some might say you don't have anything at all."

"You going to help me or not?"

Eurig gave a nod and disappeared through the mingling crowd. Bree watched him retreat, and she couldn't help but notice how the muscles in his back rippled as he moved. He was a strange one. Something in his existence as an outposter had hardened him to the rest of the realm. He liked to put on a big show, but Bree wondered exactly what he was hiding beneath his gruff and angry exterior.

Bree turned and made her way in the opposite direction. She cast her gaze around at the horned fae, sizing each one up as the potential attacker. But none of them stood out to her more than any of the rest. With their masks and their horns, they all look looked dangerous.

When Bree had first come to Underworld, she had feared these fae. They had seemed monstrous to her, and she had been certain they were capable of far worse things than the most despicable humans were. But she'd been wrong. While some of these fae were indeed full of dark things, they held the darkness far differently than humans did. They embraced it, and they learned how to use it without letting it take over their minds. The Dark Fae knew the power of the darkest parts of themselves without becoming a part of the darkness themselves.

Except for some of them, of course. Some were

just evil, but that had nothing to do with the kind of fae they were. Bree had quickly learned that there are evil beings in every realm, as well as good ones. Humans, Light Fae, Dark Fae. There are good and bad amongst them all.

A fae shoved past Bree on his way to the buffet full of a million different kinds of drinks, meats, and vegetables. Dagen had really pulled together an impressive feast for the celebration, but all of it would be for nothing now that an attack was imminent. And she needed to find him or Rafe before it was too late.

A head of thick silver hair bobbed through the crowd that surrounded the musicians who were playing a lighthearted version of the Song of the Moon Tree. The fae were all swaying to the beat, laughing and clinking their drinks as they whooped in happiness. Rafe was amongst them, looking far more relaxed than Bree had ever seen him. It made her heart hurt. His life had been just as dangerous and terror-filled as hers had been these past few weeks. She'd rarely seen him let go. It was only in those moments, those stolen ones they spent together with no one else around but each other.

And she missed that. Things had been so chaotic since the coronation that they'd rarely had a moment spent alone. And, deep down inside, she knew that things could only get worse after tonight, especially if they were not able to stop the attack.

When Bree reached him, she placed a gentle hand on his shoulder. He whirled toward her with a smile, silver eyes lit up like a full moon's sky.

"Bree," he said, wrapping an arm around her back and pulling her close. "I have been looking for you everywhere. Where have you been? You are missing the celebration."

She breathed him in, reveling in the scent of him. "Unfortunately, the celebration needs to end a little early. Fillan just showed up, Rafe. He warned me that someone plans to attack the Court tonight. Here. Now. During the ball."

Rafe's eyes slightly widened and he pulled back, dropping his hand away from her waist. "You have been speaking to Fillan? Again? I thought we warned you about the assassin. He is not to be trusted, Bree. Especially not about an attack on the Court."

"I understand that, Rafe, but he's the one who came to me." She reached out and grabbed his hand, trying to pull him back toward her. "I know he's not to be trusted, but we cannot ignore what he's told me. If there truly is an attack here tonight, it would be on us if we did not do our best to get everyone to safety."

Rafe's lips pressed together into a thin line. "You are right, even if I do not like it. Did he say anything else? Any other information that can help us know what might be about to hit us?"

"No." Bree held her breath, certain that Rafe

would react just like Conlan and Branok had. But instead of laughing and handing her a wine glass, Rafe pulled her through the crowd, away from the dancing and singing fae.

"We need to find Dagen," Rafe said. "He is a council member and the previous Hand of the King. The crowd will listen to him, and he has experience in this type of situation. In our recent history, there was more than one occasion when an angry, violent fae decided that he wanted to stage an assassination attempt on King Midas. If it wasn't for Dagen, King Midas might not have survived as long as he did."

Bree raised her eyebrows. "I thought that Midas was supposed to be the most powerful fae alive. Well, until he died, that is."

"Yes, well." Rafe lifted his eyebrows. "Even the strongest fae cannot survive everything, as was seen when Midas tried to go up against your old friend, Norah. Now, when was the last time you saw Dagen?"

Bree pursed her lips and glanced around. "Not since the celebration began. I ran into Eurig, and he took that half of the hall while I searched over here."

"You told Eurig about this?" Rafe placed his hand on the sword hanging from his belt, curling his fingers tight around the golden hilt.

"I ran into him when I was looking for you. I didn't really have much of a choice. Besides, maybe he can help us. He might be an ass, but he's strong as

hell, and most fae would not want to get in his way."
And that was putting it mildly. As much as Bree
hated to admit it, Eurig was an impressive fighter.
Hell, he didn't even need training.

Rafe's expression turned hard as he stared over
Bree's shoulder. Every single muscle in his body
looked tense, as if he were on the verge of whipping
his sword out at any moment. Bree stepped toward
him, pressing a hand to his chest. She knew how he
felt about the outposter, and she understood why.
Eurig had questioned his authority from day one,
and he probably would have let Rafe bleed out on the
ground if it'd been up to him. But despite all that,
Bree did not believe Eurig was against them. Not
truly.

"Rafe, please don't be angry at me for telling Eurig
about this. We need all the help we can get." She tried
to catch his gaze, but his eyes were too focused on
whatever stood behind her. Was he glaring at Eurig?
Had they locked eyes across the room? Was this some
strange show of masculinity? And how could she
stop it? "Come on, Rafe. Right now, we have far more
important things to worry about than what an
outposter is up to."

"Which is why that is not what I am concerned
about." Rafe slowly reached out and wrapped his
hands around Bree's wrists. He yanked hard,
throwing her behind him in one fluid motion, just as
he drew his sword.

"What's wrong?" Bree whispered, whirling to face the oncoming attackers. But when she spun on her feet, nothing was there. A few fae had fallen to the ground near the double doors, and several others were clustered around them, faces dimmed with concern.

Bree's heart thumped. Had some unseen attacker somehow sneaked in and out without being spotted? Had they lost the chance to see who it was? And what had he done to those fae? They didn't look as though they were wounded...

The fae who had gathered around the fallen suddenly collapsed to the floor, their eyes going wide and vacant in an instant. Bree clutched Rafe's hand and hovered close to his side. She didn't want him to charge into the fight, but he was out of her grasp before she could stop him. He raised his sword high in the air just as the crowd descended into chaos.

All around her, members of the Court fell to the ground. Fae after fae collapsed like mindless zombies. They didn't cry out. They didn't scream in fear. They merely fell without a sound until not a single fae was left standing.

The only one left was Bree.

CHAPTER 13
BREE

Bree stared across the Great Hall at the fallen fae, horror twisting her gut into knots. Every single fae in the massive space had collapsed onto the floor. Some were draped across the tables, across the benches, and across the stage where the musicians had fallen amongst their instruments. Their eyes were still open wide, staring unseeing at the lofted ceiling above.

She was the only one left. The only one except for... Eurig. A strange roar began to build in her chest, a roar that came from the beast deep within her. And it was directed right at Eurig.

He stood by the red tapestry that divided the Great Hall from Midas's special exit. His face was ashen, and he looked just as confused as Bree felt. But it had to be an act. Because there was no other explanation for what happened. He had done this. No one else was awake. Only him. First, he had cursed the king. And now, he had cursed the rest of the Court.

Ever since he'd come to the castle, he'd been dismissive of everyone inside of it. He was not fond of courtly ways, or of how the outposters were still pressed underneath the kings thumb, even though they had their own system of rule and justice.

Maybe he had been sent by the outposters for this very reason. Maybe he'd been sent to take the entire court down, so the outposters could finally have control over their little pocket of the realm on the sea.

Eurig's deep golden eyes locked onto hers from across the room. In an instant, it felt as if he'd read every single thought churning through her mind. He shook his head and stepped back, his body whispering against the tapestry.

"You did this," Bree whispered, her heart raging like a bull. "All this time you've been working against us, and now you've ruined it all."

She curled her hands into fists and began to storm across the room, but the fallen bodies blocked her path. She had no idea what she was going to do when she reached him, but her anger and fear were so deep that she could not stop herself from doing everything in her power to take him down.

She would make him fix this. She would make him undo what he had done. And then she would feed him to the pack of wolves that the fae of this

Court could turn into when angered. It was what he deserved.

All logical thought was drowned out in Bree's mind. She would make him pay. No matter what.

Eurig shook his head once again, taking another slow step back until the tapestry rippled from his touch. "I did not do this."

And then he was gone. He ducked beneath the tapestry and disappeared behind the sea of red. A low rumbling growl built in Bree's chest, and her feet pounded the stone ground as she chased after Eurig. Her entire vision saw red, and the bloodlust that she tried so hard to keep hidden deep within her rose up like a snake eager to strike its prey.

But as she stormed after Eurig, a familiar prone form caught her attention. It was Rafe. He laid on the ground, his bright silver eyes dimmed for once. A cry of alarm flew from her tight throat, and she came to a sudden stop beside his body. Bree dropped to her knees and placed trembling hands on his chest. Underneath her fingertips, she felt the unmistakable beat of his heart. Her entire body sighed in relief, even though there was no guarantee that she would ever be able to stare into his soul ever again.

Tears streamed down her face. She had not looked hard enough for Taveon's attacker. If only she'd done more. If only she hadn't gotten distracted by Dagen when searching for answers. If only she'd forced Fillan to tell her what was going on. She'd had so many opportunities to do more than what she had, and yet she'd squandered all that time away.

She hadn't even had a chance to kiss Rafe goodbye.

Rubbing the tears off of her cheeks, Bree leaned down and brushed Rafe's silver hair away from his slack face. The image of him was blurry through her tears, but he had never looked more handsome than he did in that moment. The emotions she felt for him were unmatched by anything she'd ever felt before. She would do whatever it took to get him back.

"Listen, Rafe. I know you probably can't hear me, but just in case you can, know that I will be back for you. I... I care for you. I'm... fond of you." Her heart lurched in her chest, the emotion she felt toward Rafe still overwhelming. There was a word she wanted to say, but not like this, not right now. She wanted to look into his eyes and see that emotion reflected back at her. And, she wanted him to truly hear her when she finally told him exactly how she felt.

She leaned down and brushed a kiss on his forehead, pressing her fingers over his eyelids. He was very much alive, his heart was beating, and his lungs were full of air. It didn't feel right leaving him like this with vacant eyes staring up at the dark ceiling.

With a ragged breath, Bree stood and picked her way across the floor to the red tapestry. She knew she would not find Eurig on the other side, but she had to check all the same. He had said that he didn't do this. Not that he would admit to it even if he had. He probably hadn't expected Bree to resist whatever curse he'd cast on the entire court. Truly, she didn't understand why she had.

There was only one person in the entire castle who might know, or at least one person that she could actually speak to, even if only in her mind.

As expected, there was no one to find on the other side of the tapestry, not even fallen fae. The corridor was quiet and dark and empty, and no guards were stationed outside of Taveon's quarters at the far end. It made Bree's heartbeat speed up even more, and a new worry twisted in her gut. If there were no guards protecting the king, and Eurig truly had been the one behind all of this, he might very well have taken this opportunity to end the king once and for all.

Bree's footsteps echoed through the corridor as she stumbled down the stone floor. The air was damp and dank, just as it always was in this castle, but now the scent carried with it a shiver of dread. Sconces lined the walls, and firelight danced. It cast shadows across the walls, fingers of darkness reaching and stretching until snapping back as she passed them by.

In only seconds, Bree reached Taveon's door. She threw it open and stormed inside, her heart jumping toward the still and silent form that laid on Taveon's bed. From a distance, she could not tell whether he was alive or dead, though she knew deep down in her gut that she would have felt it through their bond if he had left this world.

As she raced toward him, she realized that she had thrown up every barrier she had between them during the attack on the Court. Not on purpose, but instinctively, as if she'd been doing everything in her power to protect herself, to keep herself hidden from whoever had done this. But now those walls came tumbling down, and the fear and pain and anger that had been storming through her gut shot straight through the bond and into Taveon's soul.

She felt his alarm in response to her churning emotions, and the wrenching, struggling sensation of trying to push himself back into his body so he could jump up and throw his arms around Bree.

"Bree," Taveon said, his voice panicked. "What has happened? Something is wrong. Something is very much wrong. Is it Rafe? I cannot read your thoughts. They are far too jumbled..."

"Oh, Taveon," Bree said, grabbing his hand as she fell onto the bed beside him. "It is Rafe, and it is everyone else, too. The entire court has fallen prey to the curse. Dagen and I tried to throw that ball for the entire court, hoping to sniff out some information about whoever did this to you. But they retaliated instead. They cast the curse on everyone. I'm the only one left. The only one...except for Eurig."

A storm of emotions flew down the bond, emotions that matched everything Bree felt inside of her. But most of all, she could sense his guilt. Taveon thought that he could have prevented this somehow. If only he'd been strong enough to resist the curse himself.

"Are you trying to say that you believe Eurig did this?" Taveon asked, his voice full of sorrow.

"Who else could it have been?" Bree stared down at him, wondering if this was why he felt guilty about the curse. He had asked Eurig to come here, to train with Bree and Rafe. There was no way he could have known, and he was just as much a victim as everyone else.

"Eurig is a friend. I have known him since I was a boy. It is impossible to believe that he would turn on me like this, let alone that he would do this to the entire court. It must be someone else." Taveon's voice was insistent, determined, but there was a hint of doubt he tried to hide. Bree wouldn't have heard it, not normally. The bond between them meant that unintentional feelings reached her, even when he didn't want them to.

"Then, explain why he was the only one left standing."

"Not the only one, Bree," Taveon said.

Bree stiffened. "You're not suggesting that I did this, are you?"

"Of course not." Taveon reached out through the

bond, and Bree swore she could feel the caress of his hand against her cheek. "I am merely pointing out that surviving this curse does not necessarily imply guilt. You are still awake, too."

"Yeah, and it doesn't make any sense. Why would the attacker spare me? Why allow me to exist as I currently am? Eurig has never shown me anything other than disdain. And cocky disdain at that."

Taveon fell silent for a moment, as if he were thinking through everything that had happened. Several thoughts fluttered in and out of her mind, but they were there and gone too quickly for her to latch onto them.

Finally, he said, "You are not Dark Fae. You are unique. You are unlike any of the rest of us. You were once human, and now you are a version of a Light Fae. Perhaps...whatever curse was cast could not apply to you."

Bree frowned. "That might make sense, but Eurig is a Dark Fae. He's from this realm, so why wouldn't he fall prey to the curse as well? Unless he was the one who did it, of course."

"He is a Dark Fae, but he is not the same as all the rest of us. He is also unique. He is an outposter, and their biology is different than ours." Taveon sighed. "And it could also be that the curse was only meant for members of my Court. Only the Dark Fae who call this castle their permanent home. That would leave out you, Eurig, and perhaps another fae I know you have seen recently."

Curiosity fluttered through Bree, along with a large dose of confusion. What was Taveon talking about? What other fae had she recently seen?

"Fillan," Taveon said gently. "Do not forget about our bond, Bree. While you put up many walls between us at times, they often drop when you do not realize it. Mostly when you are in a moment of fierce emotion. For example, when someone is kissing you..."

Pure embarrassment poured through Bree, and her entire face filled with the heat of one million stars. Taveon knew what had happened between her and Fillan. Her walls had dropped away while she'd been kissing him. She had the sudden urge to run away and jump into the nearest hole where she would not have to come out for several years.

"Do not be so embarrassed," Taveon said, his voice still gentle. "I saw what happened. He grabbed you when you did not expect it. But I also know that you enjoyed it."

"Taveon I..." Bree fumbled for an explanation, and she wanted nothing more than to make Taveon see that the kiss with Fillan had not meant a thing. Yes, she had enjoyed it, but that didn't matter now, not when she feared Taveon would never look the same at her again, if and when she was able to bring him back into the land of the living.

"You do not need to explain anything to me Bree," Taveon said, answering words and questions that she hadn't even voiced aloud. "I do not think badly of you, and I will still look at you just as I always have. My only concern is that he is one of the most dangerous fae alive. You need to stay away from him. He keeps coming into your life, and I worry what that might mean."

"And you think that he would have survived this, too?" Bree asked, searching for a way to get the conversation away from the kiss and back onto the curse.

"Fillan is much like you and Eurig. Different. Unique. Unusual. He is something of an enigma, and I am not certain where his loyalties lie. If I were to bet, he did not fall prey to the curse either." Taveon suddenly reached out through the bond, and she swore she could feel him wrap his hand around her wrist. "I fear I should not have told you this. I fear you will search for him, and you need to stay as far away from him as possible."

"What if he has answers?" Bree asked, gently pulling her wrist out of his grip. "What if he knows information that could lead us to some kind of cure? Not to mention…"

Taveon did not know what Fillan had asked of her. He did not know that Fillan had been searching for his own answers, answers that involved Taveon's past. Was there some sort of connection? Did all of this have to do with who and what Taveon was? Bree needed to ask. She knew that Taveon was desperate to keep this information hidden not only from her but from everyone else. But she couldn't help but wonder...what if his strange past was now catching up to him?

"I know what it is you want ask," Taveon said, his voice so quiet that she could barely hear it through the bond. "But if I am going to reveal my secret to you, then it must be done face-to-face. Not like this. I have only ever told one other fae in this world, and if I am going to reveal the truth to another, I want to be able to look into her eyes when I do it."

Bree yearned to know what it was that Taveon kept locked up so tightly inside of him. She wanted to know what it was he was so scared of telling her. She knew there was a part of him that was worried what her reaction might be when she found out. Bree wanted to show him that it didn't matter. Nothing he said could change how she felt. No matter where he'd come from, no matter who he was, or what he was, Taveon would always be Taveon to Bree. She wished that he would give her the opportunity to prove her feelings for him, but she also understood his need to look into her eyes when he revealed the true depth of his nature to her.

"I understand, Taveon," Bree finally said. "But whatever it is you're hiding...are you certain that it has nothing to do with what's going on? Are you certain that it won't help me find a way to get you back?"

"I am certain," Taveon said, his voice sure and strong. "There is nothing about what I am that has anything to do with this curse. This is about the throne. Whoever is behind this wants to rule Underworld instead of me. If I were to guess, the Wilde Fae are behind this. They are likely angry about what happened at the Battle for the Crown. I would start there…though I am wary of sending you out alone. Before you go, you must promise me that you will find Eurig. And trust him. I would not tell you to go to him if I was not sure that he was on the side of good."

Bree hesitated, but not at the idea that she must seek out Eurig. She hesitated to leave Taveon. Again. She had left him so many times like this, and now she was leaving him to stew in his dark thoughts. She knew what it was like to feel powerless, and it was a feeling that she'd never wish on anyone else.

Unfortunately, she had no other choice.

Bree leaned down and kissed his cheek. He was warmer today, or maybe she'd just turned cold.

CHAPTER 14

BREE

The first order of business was finding Eurig, as much as Bree hated the thought. Taveon might be certain that his old friend had nothing to do with this, but Bree would not believe it until she found the true culprit behind the attack.

She stopped by her own quarters first and grabbed the dagger she kept hidden underneath her mattress. It was the dagger that Dagen had snuck to her during her first few days in the realm. She had never had an opportunity to use it before now, but she had a feeling that would change very soon.

She wrapped her fingers around the golden hilt and examined the engravings. Wings upon wings upon wings lined the handle, sparkling under the light of the fireplace. *Dagen*, Bree thought, her heart squeezing tight. He would be among the fallen in the

Great Hall. Before she left, she would have to check on him, even if there was nothing she could do for him, and even if there was no way for him to hear the soothing words she wished to whisper into his ear.

She felt a strange sense of loss when she thought of Dagen having fallen like all of the others. It was a feeling she hadn't expected to have. It was Dagen, after all. He had done so much against Taveon, and she hadn't been able to trust him ever since. But...he had tried to make up for it, hadn't he? And she felt so drawn to him regardless of anything else he had done. That moment they'd shared in Midas's quarters haunted her like a misty ghost just out of reach.

Did she care for him? The same way she cared for Rafe and Taveon? Surely not. Surely she was just confused. Dagen had been the enemy, or at least he had seemed to be the enemy at one point in time. His motivations had always been cloudy to her, but in the end, he'd still stood by the King's side.

As she shoved the dagger into a leather belt she had slung around her waist, the door to her quarters creaked open. She whirled, eyes wide and heart banging wildly inside her chest.

Eurig eased through the crack in the door, his hands held up high before him. "Don't stab me with that. I have not come here to attack you."

"Then, what *are* you doing here?" Bree said, slowly raising the blade up before her. "You ran off before, so why come back now?"

"Because I did not do it." Eurig took another step inside and slowly closed the door behind him, as if it made any difference. No one would hear them. No one else inside the castle had the ability to hear at the moment, except for Taveon. And he had gone silent through the bond, seeing the situation unfold through Bree's eyes.

Bree held herself steady as she stared at Eurig. "Let's just pretend for a moment that you did not put a curse on the entire court. What would be the point in coming to me now? In my opinion, the only reason you would come here now was if you *did* do it. You didn't realize that I would be immune to whatever you did. So, you've come to finish the job."

"If I wanted to finish the job, Bree, I would have come here as my shape-shifted beast. I would not be standing here, holding my hands up before you, and making myself far more vulnerable than I've ever wanted to be." He raised his hands even higher, as if to illustrate his point. "I came here to talk to you about what happened and to come up with some kind of plan going forward."

"Plan?" Bree asked, arching her brow. "You actually expect me to believe that you, of all fae, want to come up with some kind of plan to fix this? Ever since you got here, you've acted like you could not care less about this Court, let alone the King, even if he is supposed to be your friend."

"I came to this castle because I owe a favor to

Taveon. I came here to help him. He thought making me undergo ridiculous training with you would be the way I pay my debt to him. If you want to know the real reason why I have been so annoyed this entire time, it's because I felt there was so much more I can do for him than that." He shrugged. "Perhaps I was wrong for acting as I did."

"Perhaps you were." Bree lowered her dagger and shoved it into the leather belt. "Maybe you shouldn't have jumped to conclusions and assumed that training with me was so meaningless."

"You can see how I might have come to that conclusion," Eurig said. "I have been training all of my life. You have been training a few days. To say that we are on even ground would be ridiculous. I wanted to do more."

"Well, how lucky that you get to do just that."

Bree wasn't sure just how much the Dark Fae understood sarcasm, but by the look on Eurig's face, she had a pretty good feeling that he understood exactly what she meant.

"There you go again, acting as if I wanted this to happen." Eurig ran his fingers across his close-cut hair, and he began to pace from one end of Bree's room to the other. "This is as bad for Taveon as it could get. Right after his coronation, he is cursed. He is unable to do anything but lie in his bed. If it weren't for you, he would not be able to interact with anyone at all. And then his entire court falls prey to the very same curse. I would never do something like this to him. Ask him yourself. I know you can."

Bree watched him. And she couldn't help but notice that the emotion roiling off of him in waves could not be faked. Eurig might be intimidating and terrifying and a little bit rude at times, but he was not that good of an actor. She didn't *want* to trust him though. He had stormed into her Academy, acting as though he were better than everyone else. Hell, he still thought he was better than everyone else. But the Academy had become her home. It felt like hers, like hers and Rafe's. And then Eurig had come barreling in, trying to tear down everything they had built between them.

And now he was the only one in this castle that she could trust. Well, and Fillan, if the assassin had even stuck around. Bree was pretty sure he got the hell out of dodge as soon as he'd warned her of the attack.

"Why do you owe Taveon?" Bree asked. "What did he do to earn such loyalty from you?"

Eurig slowed his pacing, and he came to an abrupt stop just before Bree. As short as he was compared to the other Dark Fae, he still towered over her. His body was large and wide, like a tank, like a brick. Bree suddenly felt very small and feminine. She swallowed hard, her heartbeat racing due to nerves she hadn't expected. He clearly wasn't going to hurt her, and if he tried anything, she had more than a dagger to help her fight back. But she was nervous anyway. Why? She wasn't sure she wanted to know.

"What happened all of those years ago is between me and Taveon," Eurig muttered. "If he has not told you himself, then I cannot tell you now."

Bree raised an eyebrow, forcing back all of the questions now bubbling up in her mind. Once again, Taveon was hiding secrets. Did this have to do with his wings and his immortality? Or was there something else that he was hiding? He had told Bree that only one other fae shared his secret. No, that wasn't right. That wasn't exactly what he'd said. He said that he had only *told* one other fae. So, had Eurig somehow found out? Was that what he was now hiding from Bree, too?

"So many loyalties," Bree said, raising an eyebrow. "You were loyal enough to come here and fight for him. And you are loyal enough to hide secrets. He must have done something quite big for you. Why can't you just tell me what it is?"

Eurig drew a deep breath into his lungs, a motion that made his entire chest press out toward her. Her eyes caught on his rippling muscles and the way his shirt strained against his chiseled abs. She swallowed hard as she stared at his body, and a strange tightening sensation clenched her core. Blinking, she took a step back, wondering at what was going through her mind. She needed to get a grip. This fae was bad news, and she was only feeling drawn to him this way because the rest of the court had fallen to the ground.

"What he did for me inspired this loyalty," Eurig said, his voice sounding as rough as her heart felt. "And telling you more would reveal something about Taveon I swore I would never reveal to anyone else. So, I am afraid I cannot tell you, even knowing that it would help you trust me."

"Right." Bree sucked in a breath, trying to calm her nerves, hoping that Eurig had not noticed the pink now spreading across her cheeks. "So, am I just supposed to trust you without question then? I'm supposed to put my life in your hands not knowing why you're here?"

"You do not have to put your life into my hands for us to work together," Eurig said. "We can look into this curse. Together. As a team, just as Taveon hoped we would be one day. But you do not have to trust me in order to do that. You can keep your distance if that is what you wish to do. Just know that we would get much further if you would only open your eyes and see that I am exactly what I claim to be."

Bree just continued to stare at the outposter. He was right. They did need to work together. It was the only option they truly had. She could go out into the realm on her own, and she could try to storm the Wilde Fae villages without the help of anyone else. But deep down inside she knew it was a suicide mission. She could hear Taveon's voice in her mind, urging her to do anything but that. After everything they'd been through together, she trusted Taveon with her life. She only wished she had trusted him sooner. And it was the kind of mistake she did not want to make again.

Bree timidly held out a hand. "Okay, we'll do this together. But the second I see you do *anything* that seems even slightly suspicious, I will take this dagger, and I will put it right into your heart." Eurig stared down at her hand, slight confusion rippling across his features. In the Dark Fae realm, they did not shake hands. It was a foreign transaction, one made only in the human realm. But then Eurig reached out, his strong, warm hand wrapped around hers, and they made their pact with each other right then and there.

There were hundreds of Dark Fae in the Great Hall, but Eurig and Bree took care of as many as they could. Bree's physical strength had grown during her time spent in Underworld, through all the training she had done with Rafe. Together, they carried many of the bodies out of the hall and back to their living quarters. Some they were forced to leave as they were, but they made sure to shift them to more comfortable positions for if and when they woke up. They checked each body for wounds or bruises and tended to anyone that had been harmed during the fall.

Eurig silently helped Bree take Rafe back to his quarters and left her alone with him without even asking a question. Even though Eurig had challenged Rafe to a duel, he did seem to have a newfound respect for their instructor. And he seemed to understand that Bree had a special bond with him, a bond that was unlike any of the others that had developed during her time spent in the castle.

Her bond with Rafe was different than her magical bond with Taveon, it was different than the friendship she had found in Ethne, and it was certainly different than the strange push-pull relationship she had developed with Dagen when she had worked as his spy. Rafe was hers and she was his, even though they had made no formal commitment to each other.

With a sad sigh, Bree stared down at his prone form where he lay on his bed, now looking as if he was doing nothing more than sleeping peacefully. She dragged a finger down his cheek, remembering the way he had done exactly the same to her. She hated to leave him in the castle all alone, but if she didn't, she might never be able to find whoever had done this. And the cure. She would go to the ends of the realm if she had to.

A light knock sounded on the door, a signal from Eurig that it was time to move on. Together, they carried the rest of the council members to their quarters along with Ethne and Dagen. Through the bond, Bree sent information to Taveon, keeping him up-to-date on their movements. She couldn't bear to go to his side, knowing that she would have to leave him there once again with nothing more than his thoughts to keep him company. There was no telling how the bond would work when they were light years away from each other. Did it only work when they were in close proximity? Would it become weaker the further she traveled away from him? Unfortunately, it was time to find out.

Luckily, the horses had not fallen prey to the same curse their masters had, though they seemed to have an inkling that something was wrong. One of the stable boys had also fallen, and one of the horses had taken up residence next to him, as if she were trying to keep his body warm until he woke from his slumber.

Eurig and Bree chose two to take on the mission, but then set the others free. There was no telling how long it would be before the fae of the castle awoke, which would leave the horses alone in their stalls with nothing to eat. At least if they were free, they could graze on the land, though there were other dangers outside of the castle, like the Wilde Fae. But, right now, out there was far better than stuck inside of a castle full of ghosts.

"You ready?" Eurig asked as he sat atop a golden horse. He looked as if he belonged there, as if he had been riding all of his life.

Bree grabbed the reins of the silver horse and very unladylike slid onto the back of it. She had never been a rider in the human realm and she hadn't done much of it in the Light Fae realm either. She mostly ran on her own two feet, often in her beastly form. Truth be told, even if it meant transforming into the beast, she almost wished that was how they were traveling now.

"I thought outposters spent their entire lives on the sea," Bree said as they turned toward the front gates. "So, color me surprised that you're able to ride a horse so easily."

Eurig chuckled. "There is much misinformation about the outposters, especially being told within these castle walls. Yes, we are born over water, and we live on the sea, but we are smart enough to know that certain skills can take us far in life. And some of us have always dreamed of going further. I spent my childhood learning how to ride. My parents would take me ashore, we would ride for a day, and then we would go back home."

His voice was sad, and his eyes were distant, as if they were focused on a memory from a long, long time ago. A memory that was nothing good. Bree yearned to ask him about it. She wished to know more about his history, of his life on the sea and on the land, but he suddenly closed himself off to her, and a shutter went across all of his emotions.

"Enough about that. We better get started." Eurig flicked the reins and led the way down the stone road past the open courtyard near the front gates. The cluster of fallen guards was another sign that the curse had gone much further than the Great Hall alone. Bree couldn't help but wonder just how far it had spread. Had it gone beyond the castle? Had it gone across the entire realm? If so, Bree had no idea how they would find any answers. If there was no one else awake in the realm except for the two of them, how would they make any progress at all?

"Where are we going first?" Bree asked. "I mean, as much fun as it might be to ride aimlessly all around Underworld, maybe we should come up with a game plan."

"I thought perhaps we should check out one of the nearby villages," Eurig said, slowing his horse so that he could fall back to trot beside Bree. She was riding just a tad slower than he was. And she hoped he wouldn't be insufferable about her slower speed. "We can see if the fae who live there have been cursed as well. If not, then we will know that it was just confined to the castle."

"And if it wasn't just confined to the castle?" Bree couldn't help but ask.

Eurig fell silent for a moment, his eyes gazing at the distant horizon. "Well, then we will address that problem when we reach it. One step at a time. We do not know exactly what is happening here. Once we have a better idea, we can make a plan."

An eerie sensation whispered through Bree's gut. Eurig might pretend that he hadn't considered the repercussions, but she knew he had already imagined it, just the same as she had. Silently, they reached the front gates of the castle. Eurig jumped down from his horse to unlock the gates and push them wide open while Bree led the horses to the other side. He closed the gates behind them, even though that would do little good if the Wilde Fae came calling while they were gone.

After Eurig joined Bree back on the horses, they rode down the path that Bree had first used to reach the castle with Taveon that fateful day that felt so long ago now. In fact, it felt like years. She didn't truly know how long it had been. One month, maybe two. Three, at most. The weeks had both flown by and dragged like the chain that she'd worn when she first arrived. Indeed, it was hard to imagine a time when she had not lived in Underworld. The Light Fae realm felt distant, even while wearing her old fighting leathers, but her time as a human felt even further away than that. Like it happened to someone else, in a different lifetime.

And she guessed it had. Bree was no longer the human girl she had once been. This realm had changed her, and her life as a shapeshifting beast had changed her. The fae males she had gotten so close to had also changed her. Taveon had changed her, in the very opposite way she would have expected.

Sighing, Bree stared at the distant horizon, knowing exactly where the black rocks would lie down the path. The ring of rocks that could lead her straight back to her old life, to Otherworld, to the Light Fae she'd left behind.

It was strange, really. When she'd first come here, she wanted nothing more than to go back to the place she felt was her home. But now, she was on that road, heading in the very direction of the place Bree had fought so hard to return to. But she would not use the Faerie Ring to go back now. She would continue on past it, if that was where their path would lead. There was still too much for her to do for the Dark Fae before she went back.

"So, how far is this nearest village?" Bree asked after several long moments had passed by without a single word uttered between the two of them. Bree wasn't the kind of girl to enjoy silence for too long. She babbled nonsense if she had to, a fact that got her into trouble more often than not. "Is it far?"

Eurig cast a strange glance in her direction before he focused his attention on the horizon ahead. "I am surprised you do not know this. Has Rafferty not taught you about the villages and the geography of Underworld yet?"

Bree frowned. "Unfortunately, we got a little side-tracked when it came to that kind of training. There hasn't been much time for lessons on geography or town names or even anything related to creatures or poisons. All my training so far has been on the physical side of things. The shapeshifting, the fighting. There was the whole Battle for the Crown that we had to prepare for, and then your arrival. There's just been one thing after another. I know Taveon always planned for me to learn more than just fighting, but we just haven't had a chance to get there."

"I see." Eurig didn't seem to approve of her training, which wasn't particularly surprising. He didn't seem to approve of much of anything at all. "I understand his need to make you champion, though I cannot say I approve of how he handled it. Your lack of knowledge will make this journey far more difficult than it needs to be."

"What's that supposed to mean?" Bree asked, lifting an eyebrow as she flicked the reins in an attempt to keep up with Eurig's quick trot.

Eurig spread his arms wide, gesturing at the moonlit countryside that surrounded them. It was beautiful in a haunting sort of way. On her first journey here with Taveon, she'd been so angry, her chains rattling and her wrists stinging from pain. She hadn't paid much attention to the scenery then, but there was no denying its beauty now. The grass was silver and green, the hues lit up by the silver glow of the orb that hung low in the sky. Underworld was always cast in darkness, but the precious hours when the moon was high in the sky was often far more glorious than any daytime Bree had ever seen.

"The first village is further than a single day's ride. We will need to enter the forest first, and then make camp for the night." He shot her a grim smile. "It would have been nice for the King to teach you about the various creatures who call the forest home. Because there is no doubt that we will have to fight them at one point or another on our journey."

Bree stiffened. When Taveon had first told her about the Academy, he had mentioned sessions about poisons and creatures and flora and fauna. But the full weight of it had never truly sunk in. She had been so distracted by Taveon, so enraged by his supposed cruelty. The truth was, he had always intended to teach her more, but they hadn't reached that point yet. And now she was about to get a very hands-on lesson.

"Creatures worse than the Wilde Fae?" Bree asked with a raised eyebrow.

"The Wilde Fae are merely fae who are a bit more vicious than the rest of us. They are, simply, wild." That strange smile of his stayed locked on his face. "The creatures, on the other hand, are something else entirely. They are like our beasts, only without that extra bit of...well, I cannot say humanity because shapeshifters are not humans, but you know what I mean."

A shiver raced down Bree's spine. If the forest was truly full of creatures like Bree's beast, without the ability to shapeshift into a more human-like form, then it was chilling indeed. And slightly terrifying, though she wasn't about to admit her fear to Eurig.

"Great," Bree said, failing to keep the lighthearted tone in her voice.

"Don't worry," Eurig said with a chuckle. "I'll keep you safe."

Bree narrowed her eyes and shot Eurig a scowl. "Look, dude. I don't need you to protect me. I can certainly protect myself."

"Of course you can," Eurig said with a slight roll of his eyes. "You have seen everything this realm can throw at you while you have been tucked away in that castle of yours and your perfect little chambers with your soft bed and warm fire and all those males who want nothing more than to protect you."

Bree glared at him, tightening her grip on the reins. "Don't act like you think you know everything about me. You have no idea what I've been through, and yes, that includes my time spent in this realm. I didn't always have those chambers, you know. I was a prisoner when I first arrived, chained and locked away in a cage, like an animal in a zoo. Not that you have any idea what a zoo even is."

Oh, he was infuriating. A part of her wished she could turn around and go straight back to the castle, so she could come up with a plan to save the Court on her own. But she knew that was hopeless. As much as she hated to admit it, Eurig knew far more about the realm than she did. She wouldn't even know where to begin looking. Not that she was going to tell him that.

"I know what a zoo is. And I know what it's like to be chained and what it's like to be caged. Do not forget I am a shapeshifter like you, and my life has been far from perfect, too. You are not the only one with a sad story, Bree. You would do well to remember that."

Once again, Bree cut her eyes his way, curiosity nibbling her brain. What was his story? She hated that she wanted to know his past as much as she did. But she couldn't help herself. There was a story there. One that she felt might mirror her own, though that was impossible. How could his life have been anything like hers? He certainly didn't look any worse for wear.

In fact, he looked downright gorgeous. A fact that annoyed the shit out of Bree.

They fell silent for a while after that, the only sound the hoofbeats on the dirt path that cut through the vivid grass. As the moments stretched into hours, the moon began to dip low behind the horizon. Pinks and reds and brilliant blues lit up the sky like fireworks, and Bree couldn't help stare with her mouth slightly open in awe. She had seen a moonset once before, when Rafe had snuck her out onto the highest balcony in the highest tower. It had been brilliant then, and it was brilliant now. Different but beautiful all the same.

Eurig caught her staring, and for once, his smile seemed somewhat genuine. "Beautiful, eh? I have never seen a moonset quite like this one."

"The sunsets in the human realm are beautiful, but I have to admit they do not compare to this."

"Well, that would be because the moon and the sun are very different beasts. Darkness and light are polar opposites, but there is great beauty in both, if one looks close enough to see it."

His words warmed her, even with the chilly night air clinging to her skin. At the fork in the path, Eurig took the left path instead of going straight on to the Faerie Ring. They were headed away from the fields and toward the forest. A dark hulking monstrosity that rose up menacingly before them, like a swarm of shadows that would swallow them whole. As they grew closer and closer to the trees, the forest seemed to stretch out for miles on either side of them. Indeed, Bree swore she could not see a beginning or an end to them. The forest seemed unending, and it chilled her to think that they would soon ride straight into the very heart of it.

When they reached the tree line, Eurig brought the horse to a stop and jumped down off his steed. He motioned for Bree to do the same, taking her reins when her feet hit the ground.

Bree lifted an eyebrow and watched him get to work on building a fire with some twigs he found around the perimeter of the forest. "I thought we were going to camp out in the forest tonight. You said it was halfway from the castle to the village."

Eurig let out a low chuckle and shook his head. "It

would have been halfway if we had been riding at my speed. But you slowed us down. Besides, you know nothing about the forest. It will be safer for us to camp out here instead of in the depths of it."

Bree crossed her arms over her chest. "You don't think I have it in me. Well, I would like you to know that I am perfectly capable of going into the forest and camping out there instead of here. In fact, I insist upon it."

"Too late, Redcap Girl." Eurig threw some more twigs on top of the building pile and sunk down to his knees. "We've already stopped, and the moon will be behind the horizon within moments. It is far too late for us to ride to the next safe circle within the trees. It would take us a good two hours, and trust me, you do not want us to be riding through the forest in the dark."

Bree let out a frustrated sigh, but she could see that there was no use arguing with him any longer. He had made up his mind. And besides, as much as she wanted to prove him wrong, she knew he was right. The only evidence the moon had ever been in the sky was the slightest sliver of dark blue streaking across the horizon. Darkness loomed large, shadows clinging to everything around them. They needed to get a fire going and soon. It would be hard enough to see with the flames, much less riding on the path in this heavy of darkness, adding trees and dangerous creatures into the mix.

"Please. Continue to stand there, staring at the forest while I do all of the work for us." Eurig tossed a couple more limbs onto the pile and then made magic with some grass. Sparks shot through the darkness, and soon flames had begun to engulf the branches. Bree strode over to his side and dropped down onto the grass, staring into the flickering flames of the fire.

"What is it you would like me to do?" Bree asked, hating that she had to take second in command. But she had to admit that he knew far more about this camping out business than she did.

"Stay here and stoke the fire. I will find something for us to eat for the night." Eurig pushed up from the ground, his muscles rippling as he moved. Bree stared after him and swallowed hard, her eyes catching on every ridge of his shoulders, his biceps, and even his back through his tight tunic. He was so strong and powerful, much more powerful than she had first given him credit for.

Eurig turned and caught her look, and then a slight smile spread across his face. "Any requests?"

Bree flushed. What was he asking? Did he really think that she would make that kind of request from him? Sure, she had been appreciating his outward appearance, but she wasn't sure how she felt about the inner part of him. And besides, it was pretty rich of him to assume that just because they were traveling together that she would give that part of herself to him. Fully and completely, in a way she only ever had with Rafe.

His chuckle grew louder and deeper, and a thrill spread across her skin in spite of herself. "You need to learn a better poker face. Someone is very naughty indeed."

Bree balled her fists by her sides and glared up at him, ignoring the way the flickering fire caressed his features, enhancing his already handsome face. "Don't get so cocky. Just because I am not an idiot and I understand how the male mind works doesn't mean I want anything from you."

"Well, then it might be embarrassing for you to know that my male mind wasn't thinking anything of the sort. I was asking you what you want to eat. If you have a particular food that you like best." He winked. "I was not suggesting, as pleasant as I am sure it would be, that you should request my physical affections."

Bree's face flamed. "Good. Because I don't want your physical affections."

"Glad we got that settled." Eurig pulled a bow from his back as well as an arrow, and then he arched a single eyebrow. "So, about that request? Is there anything in particular you like to eat?"

Bree shook her head. To be honest, she did not have much of an appetite. Her gut had turned so many times during the past several hours, after witnessing all of the fallen fae inside of the Great

Hall. Carrying Rafe to his room where she had to say goodbye. Everything had happened so quickly, and Eurig and Bree had rushed out of the castle at lightning speed. It was hard to imagine eating now knowing what they had left behind.

Bree stoked the fire like Eurig had asked, anxiously awaiting his return. His warnings had put her on edge, and every crack and rustle in the forest made her jump. Finally, after several long, tense moments that felt like hours, she heard the sound of footsteps crunching through the leaves. With her heart in her throat, Bree jumped up from the ground and strode over to the tree line, peering through the thick brush toward the sound of Eurig's footsteps.

But instead of Eurig and his golden gleaming eyes, she found herself face-to-face with the red eyes of a growling beast. She could not see the full size of it, not through the thick darkness of the forest. She took one stumbling step back, and then another, fleeing to the bright glow of the fire. In the human realm, she knew that most beasts did not like fire, and she just had to hope the same would ring true in Underworld.

With a deep breath, Bree kept her gaze locked on the glowing eyes. She placed her trembling hands behind her and curled her fingers into claws. If there was one thing she had learned in her time spent training, it was how to shift, even if only one part of her body.

The beast sniffed a long shuttering type of noise that sent chills through every part of Bree. She trembled under its red gaze. She called upon her claws, picturing the way they looked carving out from large, thick, and fur-covered fingers. But nothing happened. Her fingers remained fingers instead of morphing into powerful claws.

She took another step back toward the fire, willing her body to change. The beast charged. With a roar, he was halfway toward Bree before she knew what was happening. It was then that she got a full look at him. He was nothing like she'd ever seen before. Half tiger, half bird, with fire-orange wings spread out far on either side of him. Bree stared, swallowing hard. His wings were covered in blood.

Tears sprung into Bree's eyes as she stared at the fresh blood that coated his feathers. Whoever's blood that was, they had only just been killed.

"Eurig," Bree whispered. He had gone into the forest looking for food and he must have found...*this*, whatever it was.

The beast roared, opening its hawk-like beak and emitting a noise that sounded nothing like a bird. More like a mountain lion. A massive one.

Bree clenched her jaw as she made one final attempt to transform any part of her body into the beast that lurked beneath her skin. But for once, her wolf had abandoned her. She was nowhere to be found, not when it truly counted.

And then the beast lunged. A sharp cry of alarm ripped from Bree's throat. She whirled away from the beast, pounding her feet hard against the ground. Her hair streamed out behind her, the bitter wind of the dark night fighting against her skin. She pumped her hands by her sides, forcing her feet to move as fast as they could. If only she could change her legs into the powerful limbs of her wolf, this creature who chased her would never be able to catch up.

But that wasn't happening. And she was far too slow. Something large and heavy slammed into her back, and her feet tripped underneath her. She slammed hard onto the ground and dust swirled into her face, stinging her eyes. She coughed and groaned as pain lanced through her body. Through the bond, she heard Taveon roar in agony.

Something sharp sliced through her skin, sending new shockwaves of pain through her back. The sharp, tangy scent of blood filled the air. *Her* blood. It was spilling onto the ground all around her as the beast sunk its claws into her flesh.

The world began to grow distant and tears leaked down her face as she thought of everyone she had failed. Everyone's fate had been in her hands. Taveon's, Rafe's, Dagen's. Only she and Eurig could have stopped the curse from taking its hold on the Dark Fae forever. But they had failed. They had both fallen prey to this beast. And, after tonight, there would be nothing left of them but their blood on the creature's feathers.

Just as the world dimmed into nothing more than a dark tunnel, Bree heard a different kind of roar. This one was deeper, darker, and much more powerful. And she had heard it before. It was the last thought she had before everything winked away into darkness.

✥

When Bree awoke, the scent of cooked meat filled her nostrils. Sharp pain lanced through her entire body, and her head rang from the sounds of her own distant screams. She groaned and tried to push up onto her elbows, wincing as the world tilted sideways.

He was beside her in an instant. *Eurig.* The male fae outposter who she could have sworn at one point couldn't care less whether she lived or died. "Whoa, there. You took quite a beating. You need to rest. And give your body time to heal."

"What happened?" Bree tried to think back to those last moments, to that distant memory where she'd heard Eurig's unmistakable roar cut through the bloodied night. He had attacked the beast, but she could have sworn the beast had taken him down first. If the blood hadn't been his...

"While I was hunting, I found some travelers. Or,

at least the remains of them." Eurig's face clouded over, his eyes growing distant as he stared at the fire. "And then I heard your scream. I got to you as quickly as I could. The Hawkborn is a vicious kind of creature, but he is no match for my lion."

"And he wouldn't have been a match for my beast either," Bree mumbled as a new wave of pain lanced through her. "But I couldn't shift, and I have no idea why. These past few weeks, I've gained so much control over my shift. It just left me tonight."

"The creature has the ability to control magic. He prevented you from shifting. Hell, he could have forced me to shift back into my fae form, too, if I had not caught him by surprise."

Bree cut her eyes his way, and her cheeks warmed. "Thank you. For coming to my rescue."

Eurig stiffened, clenching his jaw as he kept his gaze focused on the fire. "I did not rescue you. You would have survived, even without me. With Taveon's powers running through your veins, it could not truly harm you, at least not permanently."

Bree stiffened, her heartbeat flickering wildly. How did Eurig know that? Even at this distance, she and Taveon were still bonded together. The beast's attack would not have killed her, though it had felt like it at the time. Eurig shouldn't have known that though. There were only a few people in the realm that knew about Taveon's immortality, and as far as she knew, Eurig was not one of them.

She was tense as she glanced his way, but she tried to hide the intensity of her wariness. "What do you mean?"

He let out a chuckle and shook his head. "Now is not the time to play coy. As I said before, Taveon and I are old friends. There are things about him that I know, things that no one else knows, except maybe you. And Rafe, of course."

Bree would not speak the words aloud, just in case he was referencing something completely different than what she thought. "Okay, so maybe you're right. The bond we share gives me strength. The kind of strength that protects me. That said, the beast might have had trouble killing me, but it sure as hell hurt me far more than I've ever hurt before. And I don't know about you, but I prefer not being in intense agony."

"I have seen Taveon in intense agony before," Eurig said quietly with a nod. "So, I understand. And I would save you again and again, even knowing that you would not die."

Bree shifted toward Eurig so that she could gaze into his face, even if he still refused to meet her eyes. "One day, I hope you'll tell me what links you so strongly to Taveon. I know you say it is not your story to tell, but it sounds as though it is your story, too."

Eurig's jaw clenched tight, rippling the muscles in

his face and neck. "I am surprised that you have any interest in hearing it."

"Of course I'm interested. Whatever happened in the past has obviously made you into the fae you are today."

"Last time I checked, you were not particularly fond of the fae I am today."

"Stop being so bristly. You just came to my rescue. Don't think I don't understand that you put your life on the line just so that I would not have to suffer. Maybe I wasn't that fond of you when we first met, but people can change their minds." Bree reached out, slowly, as if she were about to touch a snake. The very tip of her finger grazed his arm. Eurig stiffened, and finally he shifted to face her.

"You would have done the same." His golden eyes glittered as he stared at her, and Bree's breath caught in her throat. He was impossibly gorgeous. She couldn't help but see it now. It was as though her eyes had seen one thing all along, but her mind had seen another. And now they were finally linked, coming together to reveal the full truth of him. And the truth was…he was one of the most breathtaking creatures she'd ever seen, his dark hair, those bright glowing eyes, and those muscles that could rival the largest tank.

"I might have done the same. Or I might have run screaming in the other direction, which…was exactly what I did when he came charging after me." Bree tried on a smile, doing her best to see the humor in the situation. Because if she couldn't laugh at herself, who could she laugh at? She might be brave at times, but she wasn't perfect. And seeing that terrifying bird lion had made every last shred of courage disintegrate into nothing more than ash.

To her relief, Eurig cracked a smile. It made his entire face light up, a fact that was highlighted by the fire that had begun to burn bright before them. She tried her best not to stare at him, though that was next to impossible. Now that she had opened her eyes to the full sight of him, it was like her mind could not shut it out. She stared at the slick skin of his neck and how his body curved perfectly over his muscles. Swallowing hard, she glanced away.

"Well, after such an eventful day, it is probably time for us to get some sleep," Eurig said, breaking the silence between them. But Bree did not want to sleep. She'd only just woken up after passing out from the attack. She knew that she needed to continue resting, as pain still lanced through her back. But she yearned for companionship. She and Eurig had only just begun to break through the barrier they'd both erected between them. Bree had a strange feeling that if she let herself drift off to sleep, everything would go back to how they'd been before the attack.

And that was the last thing she wanted to happen.

CHAPTER 16
EURIG

Eurig could tell that Bree was fighting off sleep, but it didn't take long for her body to give in to the need for rest. The poor girl had been through a lot, and it had been a hard road so far. When they had first set out on the mission together, he'd felt more than a little annoyed by her lack of experience and knowledge when it came to Underworld. But that wasn't her fault. He could see now that she had thrown herself into learning everything she could about this realm. A place that was not even her home.

With a deep breath, he stood and strode over to her side, gazing down at her peaceful expression. His heart lurched in his chest, and he had to grit his teeth against the growing affection he felt toward this female.

She was off-limits to him, as much as he hated to

admit it. Bree belonged to Taveon, and he was fairly certain she also belonged to Rafe. She had no room in her heart for an outposter, let alone one like him who had been banished from his own home.

But that didn't stop him from noting her beauty and her strength and her ferocity, a combination that could make the strongest male quake in his boots.

He leaned down and brushed a stray strand of hair away from her face. She was everything he'd ever thought he wanted, but she would never be his. If only he could have been the first to meet her. Perhaps everything would have turned out far differently than it had.

The next morning, Bree was awoken by the sound of horses. They were neighing and stomping their hooves on the ground. Bree jerked awake fast, jumping to her feet within seconds. She whirled toward the animals, who were yanking at the ropes that had kept them safely inside the clearing at the edge of the forest.

Bree turned to Eurig, confusion and panic rippling through her. What the hell was going on? What had spooked the horses? Eurig was staring at them with a frown, his hands hanging limply by his sides.

"What's gotten into them?" Bree asked. There was no one else around. There was nothing she could see that should have caused this kind of reaction in them.

"They started acting like this when the moon began to rise." Eurig's voice was edged in worry. I have done a sweep of the perimeter, checking to ensure that there is nothing lurking nearby that would cause the horses to be so afraid."

Bree raised an eyebrow. "There was nothing?"

Eurig gave a quick shake of his head. "Nothing at all. No beasts, no fae, nothing. I worry that they will bolt as soon as we untie them."

Bree frowned and glanced toward the forest. Eurig was right. The horses were so spooked that there was no way they could get them to ride on, not like this. And then a strange realization dawned in her head. She glanced at the forest, at the moonrise, and then at the horses.

"They know that we intend to ride into the forest this morning," Bree whispered. "And they are afraid. Not that I can blame them."

"But how could they know?" Eurig asked, his eyes slightly widening.

"They just know. They can see the moonrise, and they understand that we camped out here last night. The horses in the fae realm are smarter than many would believe. I saw it with my own eyes, back in Otherworld. My friend, Norah, was able to communicate with them. They understood her, and she understood them. They knew far more about how the world worked than I ever would have imagined."

Eurig let out a heavy sigh. "If that's the case, then we truly cannot continue forward. Not on horseback anyway."

"Then, I guess that means we have to walk." Bree knew how it sounded even before she spoke the words aloud. Crazy, especially considering the beasts that haunted this forest. But Bree had started this mission, and she was determined to finish it. She had to find answers, and the only way to do that was to keep moving forward.

Eurig didn't respond, but he didn't argue either. Instead, they gathered up their supplies in silence, taking what they needed from the bags slung across the horses. Strangely, it was if the animals understood their change of plans, as they ceased their neighing and their stomping and fell still and silent while Eurig and Bree collected everything they could carry themselves. When they were ready to leave, Bree untied the horses and took a step back just as they stormed away from the perimeter of the forest. She could not blame them, really. Bree might have Taveon's power of immortality, but the horses didn't, and she did not want a single creature to perish needlessly.

"This is going to be one hell of a walk," Eurig said as they finally stepped foot into the thick forest that held so much darkness and fear. "The village is probably two more days on foot from here. We could have reached it within hours on horseback but now we will have to camp at least one more time in the middle of this web."

"Luckily, you have me," Bree quirked with a bright

grin that didn't match the churning in her stomach. "When beasts attack, I can use my powers of screaming and running away to fight them."

Bree meant it as a joke, but Eurig didn't seem to find it funny. He pressed his lips together, the pink skin turning white with the pressure. "You are only invincible because of the bond you share with Taveon. We do not know how far that bond stretches. Don't get too cocky. We don't want to find out the hard way that your connection to him only works when you're in close proximity."

"So," Bree said with a wince, desperate to change the subject. "We didn't have a chance to talk about those travelers you found. How did they look when you came across them? Were they...aware, awake?"

"You mean to ask if they'd been affected by the curse." Eurig shot a sideways glance her way, hoisting the heavy bag higher onto his shoulder. "I wondered the same thing when I came upon them. It could be the answer we need, without going further into the forest. Unfortunately, their bodies were too mutilated by the beast for me to tell whether they'd been alive and awake when he'd come upon them."

"Damn." As horrible as the incident had been, it could have given Bree and Eurig some insight into how far the curse had permeated throughout these lands. She should have known when he'd said nothing about it, when he'd insisted they keep moving forward with their plan to trek through the forest that held so many dangerous creatures, creatures that Bree did not know how to fight.

"That said, they were not merely helpless travelers. They all had swords and bows and arrows. As far as I could tell, not a single arrow had been fired. It did not look as though they had tried to fight back, which would suggest…"

Bree tightened the grip around the bag handle that dug heavily into her shoulder. "It sounds like they were affected by the curse."

"There's no way to know for sure, but it certainly seems that way." Eurig suddenly stopped, wrapping his strong hand around Bree's arm and yanking her close to his side. Her heart trembled, but not from fear. She couldn't help but notice that his hands were so large that his fingers encircled her arm completely, the tip of his thumb curling over the tip of his shortest finger. She could feel the warmth of his touch through her thin tunic, lighting up a fire that blazed right in her belly.

"What is it?" Bree asked, her voice more ragged than she'd intended.

"I thought I heard something," Eurig said, cocking his head. "Did you not?"

Bree stiffened and scanned her eyes across the thick forest, but the trees were far too tightly clustered for her to see anything more than bark, branches, and brush that weaved together into a tapestry of green. "No. But when I became a Light

Fae, I wasn't lucky enough to get some of the more enhanced powers, like a better sense of hearing. If you heard something far away in the distance, then unfortunately I wouldn't have been able to myself."

Eurig stayed frozen for another solid minute before shaking his head and letting go of her arm. Bree stared down at the place where his fingers had encircled her skin, and a strange part of her yearned for that hand to be on her once again. "It's probably nothing. This forest is home to a million different sounds and smells. If it was something dangerous, then we would definitely know by now."

Bree shivered, even with his reassurance that nothing was wrong. Just the idea that something might be out there, watching them, was enough to send chills deep into her bones.

Eurig and Bree continued onward for what felt like years. The entire forest looked exactly the same. Tree after tree after tree, leaves all glowing with silver and green. They managed to make it all the way to their clearing without any incidents or any sign of dangerous beasts. Eurig got started on the fire while Bree gathered some more wood to last them through the night. He was insistent that nothing would bother them, not as long as they kept the fire going. But Bree wasn't convinced. That half bird creature had attacked when she'd had the fire blazing behind her. What was to stop another one from doing just the same?

Still, she did what he'd asked. And once the fire was going and they'd settled in on the blankets with swords in their hands, Bree finally felt her body relax. Eurig mysteriously pulled some meat from his bag, and Bree did not want to ask where it had come from. Deep down inside she knew. He had killed the half bird creature who had attacked, and he'd prepared the meat while she'd been resting. Together, they got to work on roasting the bird, and Bree hesitantly reached out through the bond toward Taveon.

She loosed a sigh of relief when he was waiting there for her on the other side, just as vivid and as real as he'd felt back at the castle. So far so good. Their bond still stood tall, keeping them linked together even across this distance.

"Bree," Taveon whispered down the bond, his voice caressing her frazzled nerves. "Where are you? Are you okay? Have you healed after the attack?"

Bree smiled at him, hoping he could read her expression. "I know you don't need to ask me those questions for you to know the answers. I'm fine, Taveon. Our bond kept me safe. So did Eurig. He killed the beast before it could do any more damage."

"I want you to come back. This is far too dangerous. I do not want you risking your life for me."

"Taveon, I..."

"That is not a request, Bree. It is in order. From your King." Taveon's voice was hard and full of ice, a tone he'd rarely used since revealing the truth of himself to Bree. It was the tone he liked to use when he wanted to hide his true emotions from whoever he was talking to. He'd used it with Bree when she had first arrived in Underworld, hoping that his harshness would push her away. But he should have known better by now. He was not harsh, he was not hard, and he was not cruel. Behind his words, she could feel the truth of his emotions through the bond.

He was scared as hell, and he did not know how to help Bree other than to use his status as King, hoping she would listen to his order.

"Taveon," Bree said gently. "You know I'm not going to turn around now."

"You do not even know if you are going to find answers in this village. Come back to the castle. If you insist on trying to help, we can form another plan. It is not safe for you in that forest."

"It is already past the set of the moon, Taveon. It would be more dangerous to trek back now when it's dark."

"So then come back first thing in the morning."

"We will reach the village tomorrow. We must press on." Bree reached out a hand through the bond and tried to wrap it gently around his, feeling his essence underneath her fingertips. "I know you're worried about me, Taveon, but nothing can harm me as long as we are linked."

"You know that is wrong," Taveon said. "Yesterday, the beast harmed you. You may be immortal, but you can feel pain just as easily as anyone else. Just like me. And I know how terrible the pain can be. If the wrong beast got ahold of you, it would tear you to shreds and continue to do so until your soul left your body. But your soul would remain. The pain would just continue and continue and continue..."

Fear churned through Bree's gut, but she did her best to hide it from Taveon. Indeed, it was a terrifying thought, but one she refused to dwell on right now. There was no turning back now. Not only for Taveon but for Rafe and Dagen and the entire Court.

Taveon must have felt her determination through the bond because he fell silent. Moments passed with no more sound but the flickering fire as Eurig leaned over it, turning the wood over the flames. But then Taveon's voice sounded loud once more in her ear. "Very well. But you will return to the castle as soon as you discover what has happened in the village. Ride through the forest as fast as you can. No more camping there. I will not allow it."

Bree had to smile. He might not be the true-born son of King Midas, but he was a King all the same.

"You look like you're in some kind of trance," Eurig said when she moved to his side after throwing up a slight wall between her and Taveon. "Were you talking to my old friend, then?"

"Did I really look like I was in a trance?" Bree asked. She never considered her expression when speaking to Taveon through the bond, but Eurig had a point. It probably looked weird, seeing Bree do nothing more than staring off into space with eyes distant and mind somewhere completely other than where she currently was.

Eurig gave a nod. "I hope everything is still well at the castle?"

"It would seem so. But who knows?" Bree sighed and wrapped her arms around her knees, pulling them close to her chest. "He tried to order me to go back. He is not a big fan of the two of us spending the night in the forest."

Eurig let out a low chuckle. "That's because Taveon is not an idiot. To be honest, I'm not a big fan of the two of us spending the night here either."

"Do you think one of those creatures will attack us again?" Bree asked, trying to keep the fear out of her voice. She didn't want Eurig to know just how terrified she was to face another monster, especially if she was not able to face it in her own beastly form. Even though they had struck up something akin to friendship, she still felt the need to put on a show of strength in front of him.

Eurig rubbed his jaw, causing Bree's gaze to snap onto the chiseled curves of his face. The firelight illuminated his sharp cheekbones and the full jaw that jutted out like a towering cliff. "Unlikely. That said, we need to be on our guard. It is never a good idea to relax in this forest." He cut his eyes her way and the ghost of a smile flickered across his lips. "Are you actually admitting that you're nervous? The great, brave Bree?"

Bree shot him a scowl. "Of course I'm not nervous. I'd just rather get some sleep than have to deal with a monster tonight."

"If you say so." The smile didn't drop from Eurig's face. That smugness. That righteousness. It irritated the hell out of Bree.

As the night deepened, Bree and Eurig took turns keeping watch over their makeshift camp in the middle of the forest. But even during her stint on the ground, with her cheek pressed against the cool dirt, Bree could not find a single moment of blissful slumber. Everything about the night had her on edge. She was all too aware of every crack in the forest. Every hoot of an owl. And every whistle of wind through the trees. And, she was far too aware of Eurig's presence. She could hear his every sigh and smell the intoxicating scent of him every time the wind brushed past him. Mint, cinnamon, and sea. Her body was tense, and she wanted nothing more than to jump from the ground and pace back and forth until the moon rose high in the sky.

Not that she could let him know that.

When dawn finally came, Bree's eyelids felt heavier than an elephant's hoof. Her body ached from exhaustion from that tightly held tension that had kept her awake every moment of the night.

Eurig, on the other hand, looked irritatingly bright-eyed and bushy-tailed. When Bree stood and brushed the dirt from her leathers, Eurig gave her a full-length gaze, and then he raised his eyebrows.

"You look as though you've just spent the past eight hours on horseback instead of resting on the ground. Are you still recovering from the attack?"

Bree bit her lip. "Right. The attack. Yep, I'm still recovering. It made it kind of hard to fall asleep last night."

Eurig still stood there gazing at her with raised eyebrows. "Why didn't you say something? I could have tried to put a sleeping draught together for you. There are plenty of plants in these woods that could have helped."

"And have you stomping around in the bushes in the dark and alerting every creature of exactly where we are?" Bree let out a tense laugh. "Yeah, that was not my top choice in how to spend the night."

In the distance, branches cracked. Bree froze at the sound, her entire body going on high alert. The echo of crackling twigs was not far different than the dozens of others sounds that echoed throughout the forest, but Bree knew deep down in her gut that it was not the same. There was something more purposeful about these cracks. Like they were the result of approaching footsteps. Footsteps aimed right at their camp.

Eurig met Bree's gaze across the fire, and he

motioned for her to move to his side. Swallowing hard, she joined him on the opposite side of the flames, reaching to her belt for the dagger she kept tucked in its folds.

He jerked his head, and then pointed to her fingers and teeth.

Bree understood in an instant what he meant. He wanted her to shift into her wolf in order to fight. Her heart raced at the thought. If that were the case, then whatever was out there must be far more terrible than she wanted to imagine.

By her side, Eurig's body was already twisting and shuddering into his lion-like form. Closing her eyes, Bree quickly undressed and followed suit. Her beast was eager to get out, its soul yearning to join the fight. It had been forced to take a backseat the night before, and now, it wanted nothing more than to rip the attackers to shreds.

Just as soon as her claws had fully extended before her, a half a dozen snorting creatures hurtled toward them from all corners of the forest. They landed in the clearing, their sharp, glinting fangs dripping with reddish saliva. It was a sight that made Bree's stomach turn and one that made her beast bellow in rage.

They were half her size, but they were monstrous all the same. They launched onto her back, digging their sharp little claws into her skin. Pain lanced through her body, and the beast screamed in rage.

She twisted and turned, trying to shake the creatures from her back. But still, they clung on.

Several others had launched themselves onto Eurig's back, and one had bit a chunk out of his shoulder. Out of the corner of her eye, she could see them pile on top of his form. They had pinned him to the ground, and Bree was no better off than he was.

They were going to lose. The creatures were going to win.

But then Eurig roared. The sound echoed through the forest and sunk deep into Bree's bones. The creatures began to fly, Eurig's strength returning to him in a flash of glory. He grabbed one after another and launched them through the air where they slammed into thick tree trunks or tumbled with a heavy thump onto the ground.

Bree's face was smashed into the dirt, and she watched it all unfold with only one eye open. The pain in her back was far too unbearable for her to do anything else.

When Eurig finally turned her way, she could have sworn she saw something akin to fear flash in the lion's eyes. But that was impossible. Eurig did not truly care what happened to Bree, especially not in his lion form. He was only helping her because of Taveon. He probably thought he'd be better off without her in his way.

But then he stormed over to her, plucking the creatures from her back and snapping them in two.

He threw them into the forest, and the crack of their bodies against the trees made her stomach twist into knots. Soon, the pain was the only thing left. That and Eurig, who stood beside her with wild eyes and bloodied claws.

CHAPTER 18

BREE

Bree watched Eurig slowly transform back into his fae form. His limbs twisted, his bones cracked, and his face twisted into brutal agony. Her heart pounded in her chest as she watched the hair on his arms slowly slide into his skin as if they were knives being sheathed. Was this what she looked like? Is this what her body did when she made her own transformation? Bree had never watched her own shift. She wouldn't be able to. In her head, she had tried to imagine what it looked like, but her imagination had not conjured anything as quite as violent and gruesome as this.

After several long moments where Bree felt as though she wanted nothing more than to reach out and place a hand on Eurig's shuddering shoulder, he was finally back as himself, one fist braced on the dirt as his body curled over it. Despite herself, Bree couldn't help but gaze at him. His muscles trembled and his skin was slick with sweat. As he stared down at the ground, his back was turned toward her. Red marks crisscrossed down the entire length of him. Wounds. No, scars. Ones that looked both old and ancient as well as new.

Slowly, Eurig lifted his eyes to meet her gaze. His voice was rough when he spoke. "I suppose you're wondering what these are all about." He jerked his thumb behind him, clearly referencing the multitude of scars on his back. "I had not meant for you to see them, at least not for a while. They are not something I'm proud of."

Bree lowered herself to the ground, her knees now digging into the dirt, just like his. "Why would you be ashamed of them? We all have scars. Some are just more obvious than others."

"Because they are a constant reminder of the weakest parts of me and what I was unable to do to save my family."

Bree lifted an eyebrow, and her breath stilled in her lungs. "What happened, Eurig? Who gave you these scars?"

Eurig let out a long, hollow sigh, one that shuddered through his entire body. "It is such a long story. I do not want to bore you."

She grasped his hand in hers and squeezed tight.

"Stop it. You will not bore me. I want to know what happened to you."

"Fine." His jaw rippled as he clenched his teeth together. "If you truly wish to know, then I will tell you. But let me tend to your wounds while I do."

Bree felt that Eurig was the one who needed to be tended to, not her. While she had a few cuts and gashes sprinkled across her skin, it was nothing compared to the deep gouge in Eurig's shoulder. Her bond with Taveon would ensure she healed. Eventually. Eurig? He didn't have that luxury. But despite her protestations, he insisted on looking at her wounds first.

Eurig grabbed a rough blanket from their rucksack and draped it around Bree's legs as he settled in behind her. As he moved, her eyes flicked across every inch of his exposed skin. He didn't seem the least bit self-conscious, even though he was fully naked before her. Her own cheeks were flushed from the heat of her embarrassment. She wasn't wearing a damn thing either. Not that he seemed to notice, a fact that disappointed Bree far more than she would have expected.

His strong, rough fingers trailed across her back, and she shivered underneath his touch. He gathered her hair in his hand and gently brushed it away from her skin so that it dropped over her shoulder and spilled across her chest. Her entire body trembled, and she could not stop her heart from thundering like the hooves of a frantic horse. A part of her yearned to twist her head to look over her shoulder at Eurig, but she couldn't bring herself to do it, not trusting how she would react if their faces came so close to one another. So, instead, she merely swallowed hard and kept her eyes focused on the dirt-packed ground beneath her.

"The cut here is quite deep," Eurig said softly as he gently poked a finger at her wound. Pain shot through her back, and Bree winced. "I'm sorry. I did not intend to hurt you."

"You're not the one who hurt me, Eurig. You're the one who saved me. Again." Bree sucked a deep breath into her lungs and winced when Eurig's hand traveled south toward another one of her cuts. "I thought I was improving with the whole fighting thing, but if this has shown me anything, it's that I have way more training to do if I want to be useful to Taveon."

"I daresay that Taveon would not agree. It seems that he understands what you are worth, even if you do not."

Bree's heart warmed, as well as her cheeks. She hated that the outposter had this kind of effect on her, but there was no stopping it at this point. She may have distrusted him when they'd first set out on this mission, and she certainly hadn't liked him, but a lot had changed in only a couple of day's time. Now, she couldn't help but yearn to know him. To *really* know him.

"Speaking of knowing your worth, I think we had an agreement. I let you check out my wounds, and you promised to tell me about your scars."

Eurig's hand stilled on her back, and she heard a sharp intake of breath. "Very well. We did have an agreement. Where would you like me to begin?"

"At the beginning."

Eurig let out a harsh chuckle. "If I started at the very beginning, we would be here all night and all day and for many nights and days far after."

Bree wouldn't say it aloud, but that didn't sound like a terrible proposition to her, not with his strong and warm hands on her back.

"I will start with our previous ruler. King Clarke. He ruled the outposts for many centuries. He was very loved, but he was not feared. In fact, he was so loved that many believed the outposters would never see another ruler, not for many, many long centuries. Unfortunately, being loved wasn't enough. One of our kind rose up against him and killed him while he sat on his throne."

Bree gasped. Not because she found it difficult to believe but because she could have so easily guessed that was where Eurig's story was headed. This realm, as beautiful as it could be, was full of so much death.

"Her name was Queen Freya. She was the King's

wife, but she had never been able to give him an heir. His death meant that she took his place on the throne, despite the hate and anger all of the outposters felt toward her because of what she'd done."

As Eurig told his story, he spread something soft and cool across Bree's wounds. A strange new sensation of warmth shot through her core, but this time, it was different. It had nothing to do with Eurig's touch and everything to do with whatever magic he was rubbing into her skin. This salve was healing her.

"But even though King Clarke had no legitimate heirs, he had at least a dozen bastards." Eurig's voice went hard and rough, reminding Bree of the look in his eye when he often stared at the horizon, his mind somewhere far away and in the past. "I was one of these bastards. I mean, I *am.* Not was. I will always be his son, and the new queen knew that. And I was his eldest. She worried that the outposters would want me to become the ruler instead of her. She killed the other bastards, and then she took me prisoner. She would have killed me, too, but Taveon convinced his father to make the new queen a deal. And so she set me free."

Bree's heart roared in her ears, and she twisted to face Eurig, catching the crumpled expression on his face. "That is why you are so loyal to Taveon."

Eurig gave a quick shake of his head. "That is part of it, but that is not all of it. You wanted to know how I got my scars. This is how. While the Queen kept me prisoner, she made sure to remind me of exactly where I stood in the grand scheme of things. So, she had me tortured. I was nothing. Nothing but an ant she could stomp out whenever she wanted. Truth be told, I still am."

Bree stared at Eurig. He was far more than an ant, far more than nothing. If anyone was going to be stomping on anyone else, it would be him and not a queen who had killed her own husband in order to take control of the outposts on the sea. Bree swallowed hard, and she reached her hand out to Eurig, letting the tips of her fingers brush against his leg. She'd known that he'd experienced something in his past, but she'd never guessed it was quite as terrible as this.

Eurig's gaze locked on where Bree's fingers brushed against his skin, and a fierce heat sparked in his eyes. She stared at his chest, at the tightly-coiled muscles that rippled as he moved. She drank in his shoulders, his jaw, and those lips that looked as though they could turn any female into a writhing mess.

"You know that you should not let your Queen define who and what you are." Bree sucked in a deep breath, forcing herself to be a little bit braver. She shifted her hand even closer, sliding her fingers further onto his leg. "You are one of the strongest fae I've ever met. The only one who could ever beat you in a fight is probably Taveon, but only because he has that special gift of his. He could only beat you because he cannot die."

A slight smile lifted the corners of his mouth, and he lifted his gaze from Bree's hand until he looked into her eyes. "You believe Taveon could beat me?"

Bree licked her lips and swallowed hard. "Couldn't he?"

"It depends on what kind of fight we are waging." Eurig's hand suddenly appeared over hers, and his fingers slid between her own. His eyes were full of heat, and his words were laced with suggestion. Or at least she thought it was suggestion. Maybe he was just teasing her, like he had done at least a dozen times already.

But then he leaned closer to her, bringing his face only an inch away from hers. She breathed him in, and the scent of cinnamon, mint, and the sea enveloped her. Her heart rattled in her chest, and her whole body felt tense, as if she were about to jump off the edge of a very tall cliff.

Eurig reached up, and he brushed a thumb against her cheek. Bree practically moaned from the sparks that shot through her. "How are your wounds feeling?"

He wanted to talk about wounds right now? The pain was the last thing on her mind, not when both of them were sitting so closely.

"They're fine," she squeaked out, her eyes locking on his full lips.

He dropped his forehead against hers. Closing his eyes, he sucked in a deep breath, and then he said the words that knocked Bree straight out of the moment and back into reality. "Good. You should get dressed. We need to make our way to the village."

They were silent during the rest of the trek to the village. Bree had nothing to say, her mind too wrapped up in their almost close encounter. She couldn't decide whether or not she was the one being crazy. Had she imagined the tension between them? Was her desire for him one-sided? For a moment, it seemed as if he was just as drawn to her as she was to him, but then he had pulled away. Hell, he'd acted as though he didn't even see her in that way.

They'd been naked. They'd been alone. And they'd practically been sitting on top of each other. If he didn't want to take her then, then she didn't see how or why he ever would. It had been the perfect moment, and now it was gone. Unfortunately, it just made Bree want him even more.

Soon, the trees began to thin before them. Eurig

had filled Bree in on what to expect from the village. It was a small little town, one that could barely be called that. It had been erected in the center of a small clearing in the forest centuries and centuries ago, surrounded by a magical barrier that protected each inhabitant from the creatures that roamed through the night. While the fae could come and go whenever they pleased, no monsters could creep into their midst.

But their location in the forest meant that they rarely left the safety of their walls. They were hermits, loners, and they were not fond of visitors, even ones who would come from the King. They would not be happy to see Bree and Eurig, nor would they be likely to provide them with a warm bed for the coming night. The two of them would need to assess the situation and leave as quickly as possible, aiming to get out of the forest as soon as they could.

Of course, that would only be the case if the villagers were actually free of the curse. And Bree wasn't feeling particularly optimistic.

Leaves and limbs crackled underfoot as they made slow steps toward the village. Buildings began to blur in before her, built from the wood of the trees all around them instead of the stone that had built the castle beyond. The village turned out to be nothing more than a small cluster of buildings. Maybe eight in total. In the dim lighting, Bree could make out what appeared to be a pub, a blacksmith, and a mill, while the other buildings looked like small homes, quaint little cottages with only a room or two.

Bree dropped her voice into a whisper, just in case the residents of this village were somewhere nearby, even if they could not be seen. "How many fae live here?"

"About twenty in total." Eurig gave a nod toward the cluster of small homes. "All families. Mothers and fathers, daughters and sons. They rarely get any new villagers moving here, and the ones who grow up here rarely leave. Much like the outposts."

Bree raised an eyebrow. She still knew very little about Eurig's life back on the sea, but she also knew that he didn't want to be pressed too hard about it. "How many fae live in the outposts?"

"Oh, far more than live here." Eurig pressed his lips into a thin line. "There are thousands of outposters. So, in that regard, my world is nothing like this one here. But it is still the same in a way. No one ever leaves, and no one ever comes."

Bree jerked her head toward Eurig and raised her eyebrows. "Thousands? I had no idea there were that many outposters. I thought there would be maybe fifty. One-hundred, tops. But thousands? How do you all live on the sea?"

Eurig pursed his lips, and then shot her a wink. "You do realize that the sea is a very large expanse of water, yes? It is much larger than this continent on which you stand. Over the centuries, the outposters have built thousands of platforms that dot the waters, a maze of homes and paths that rise up above the sea. It is…impressive."

"It sounds impressive. I wish I could see it." It sounded unlike anything Bree had ever laid eyes on. It was certainly nothing like any city found in the human realm, and as far as she knew, there was nothing like it in the Light Fae realm either.

"If I could take you, I would," Eurig said, the smile dropping off of his face. It was replaced with that sad expression he wore so well. "But I am no longer welcome there. Not in my own home. The Queen let me go free, but doing so meant that I was banished from the outposts. Taveon may have gotten me my freedom, but there was nothing he could do to keep my home in my hands."

Bree's heart hurt. She knew how he felt. She'd been ripped from her home, too, though time had begun to heal that wound. Her human home no longer felt like the safety of a warm blanket, a large mug of tea, and a roaring fireplace. She glanced down at her fighting leathers, a reminder of the Light Fae realm that she carried with her wherever she went. That realm had felt more like her home than New York City ever had. And she'd been ripped away from it, too.

But unlike Eurig, Bree could go back. She had not been banished, and she would not be turned away if she walked up to the castle and asked to rejoin the court.

One day. She would return, but just not yet.

"Nothing lasts forever," Bree finally said. "That Queen may rule the outposts now, but one day, she will fall."

Eurig shook his head. "Even if she does, I doubt the outposts will ever again be my home. I have changed. The realm has changed. Returning would be like stepping back in time, and I only want to move forward now. Fate has decided to bring me here. So be it."

Bree and Eurig fell silent as they came to a stop in the middle of the village square, the dirt-packed ground hard underneath their feet. They both gazed around them, drinking in the quiet buildings, the empty mill, and the lack of any vibrant displays of village life.

"This is not a good sign," Bree said quietly, her heart skipping a beat. Even though it was a small village, there should be at least some sign of life. The sound of voices. The clink of dishes. Or the soft padding of footsteps against the ground. There was none of that. The tiny little village felt like a ghost town.

Eurig's body went tense, and he rested his hand on the bow strapped to his back. "We will check out the buildings together. Let's start with the pub. If there are any fae still awake this night, at least one would be there."

Bree gave a nod, swallowing back the desire to suggest they split up. She knew just as much as he did that it was a terrible idea. They had been attacked twice. And even though this village was protected by magic, it did nothing to stop a fae from entering. A fae that might have cursed everyone in his or her path.

Slowly, they eased up the rickety stairs of the pub. Eurig stepped just in front of Bree, his bow and arrow drawn. When they reached the door, he kicked it open. The wood splintered with a loud crack, and shards rained down on the ground. Bree braced herself for cries of alarm or some kind of retaliation from the fae hidden within, but nothing came.

Eurig stepped into the pub, and Bree followed just behind. Inside, they found three bodies sprawled across the floor. Two males and a female, all with half-full tankards on the tables just beside them. Their eyes were open, and they gazed un-seeing at the ceiling.

Bree had seen this before inside of the Great Hall. They looked cursed.

Eurig lowered his bow and crossed the room in two massive steps. He dropped to the ground beside the female and pressed his fingers against her neck. His breath shuddered from his lungs as he gave a nod. "She is alive."

A relief, but one filled with dread all the same. She might be alive, but that meant the curse had extended far past the gates of the castle. It extended all the way out here into the Forest of the Fireflies. There was no telling how much further it went. If this village had fallen, had the next? And the next? Were there any non-cursed fae left inside this realm other than Eurig and Bree?

"So, now we know," Bree said, her voice tight in her throat. "But what do we do now?"

Eurig slowly stood, lifting his bow before him once again. "We check the other buildings, including the homes. Perhaps we can find some answers there."

Bree gave a nod, but she wasn't so certain. Eurig had insisted they scour the castle before they left, and they had found nothing inside of the Great Hall to indicate what had happened. She didn't see how they would find anything now either. Whoever had done this had likely done it from afar, leaving behind no evidence of their treachery. They would only find more bodies, more cursed fae lying fallen on the ground.

But she saw no need to argue. If Eurig wanted to take a look around, then she would do nothing but help.

They left the pub and moved to the blacksmith's building. Inside, everything had been thrown into chaos. Chairs had been splintered against the wall, and tables had been overturned. There were no weapons and no armor in sight. It looked as though the place had been ransacked.

Bree sucked in a sharp breath and whirled toward Eurig, who was gazing at the mess with as much shock as she felt. "How could this have happened? Do you think whoever cursed these fae actually came here and took their weapons? I just assumed they'd cursed everyone from afar."

Bree's heart thumped hard. If that were the case, then the fae behind all of this had far worse intentions than any of them had dared to believe. They needed to get back to the castle as soon as they could. If the attacker–or attackers—had come here, then there was no doubt they would head to the castle, too.

Eurig shook his head, eyes still wide. "I have seen this before. This kind of chaotic ransacking. This looks like the work of the Wilde Fae."

Those were words that Bree had hoped she wouldn't hear. It was one thing to face off against a solo assassin, one who was trying to pick off members of the court slowly and methodically. But to imagine that they were up against all of the Wilde Fae...she did not know how they would win. Bree and Eurig were only two. The Wilde Fae were legion.

Out of the corner of her eye, several black forms caught her attention. She twisted toward them, eyeing the feathers that dotted the floor. She took several steps toward them, following the path of feathers. They led her around a far table that had not been tipped over. Just behind it, she found three dead ravens in a pool of tarry blood. Chills swept across her skin, and her breath stilled in her lungs.

Bree had found a dead raven in her bed just after Taveon had fallen at the coronation. And now, there were three inside this building. It couldn't be a coincidence. These dead ravens must mean something, but what?

"What's wrong?" Eurig asked, striding up behind her and placing a warm soothing hand on her shoulder.

Bree stepped back and took comfort in the solidness of his chest. She shook her head and swallowed hard, her eyes still locked on the birds. "To be honest, Eurig, I don't know. But if my gut instinct is right, these ravens are a sign of something far worse than we thought."

CHAPTER 20

BREE

While Eurig moved the fallen villagers into their beds, Bree found a stool inside of the pub, climbed on top of it, and reached out through her bond to Taveon. After everything they had discovered, she was desperate to hear his voice. Besides, they needed to fill him in on what had happened. Bree might not understand what the ravens meant, but Taveon might. And it might just be the clue they needed to unlock this entire thing.

"Bree," Taveon said, his voice sharp with worry. "Please stop putting up so many walls between us. I have been worried out of my mind, scared that something else attacked you. Here and there, I felt pain shooting through the bond, and fear, as well as sorrow. What has happened? Are you all right?"

Bree closed her eyes, battling the storm of

emotions that shook through Taveon's soul. Her own emotions were heightened just from the contact with his mind. If he wanted to know why she kept up the walls, this was why. As much as she yearned to be close to him, it was still far too much.

"We made it to the village," she said without bringing up the second attack in the forest. There was no reason to worry him any more than she already had. "Just as we worried, the curse hit here, too. All of them have fallen, and the buildings have been ransacked, especially for weapons."

Bree fell silent, giving Taveon a chance to weigh her words. And he came to the same conclusion that Eurig had.

"Ransacked? That sounds like the Wilde Fae to me."

"Yes, it does." Again, Bree let her words sink into Taveon's mind. She knew how he would react when he discovered what was on her mind, but she would not back down. No matter what he said. No matter that he was the King. Bree knew what she needed to do, and nothing would stop her.

Taveon read all the thoughts fluttering through her mind, and he raged against them. "No. I will not allow it, Bree. You and Eurig cannot storm the lands of the Wilde Fae alone. There are only two of you, and they will kill you on the spot. They know who you are. My champion. The fae who defeated one of their own."

"None of that matters now, Taveon," Bree said quietly. "They have clearly planned something, and it involves you and everyone inside of the Court. If Eurig and I do not take them down, there is no telling what they will do next."

In fact, they were likely to storm the castle. With everyone inside of it under that curse, there would be no soldiers or guards or fighters there to stop them from taking complete control of the throne. They might even kill everyone there, including Rafferty, Dagen, Ethne, and Taveon. Bree could not let that happen.

"I appreciate your bravery, Bree," Taveon said, his voice growing more panicked by the moment. "But this is senseless. It will solve nothing. The two of you cannot win against hundreds or thousands of Wilde Fae."

"Then, our plan better be a hell of a good one, don't you think?" Bree asked with a hollow laugh. "Don't worry. We're not just going to run in there with swords swirling through the air. We'll be stealthy. Covert."

"I do not like this, Bree."

"Too bad," Bree said, curling her hands around the edge of the stool. "Because I'm going to do it whether you like it or not."

At that, Bree threw up every wall she could. Deep down, she hated breaking Taveon off like this, especially knowing that he had no one else in the world that he could speak to right now. But Bree also knew that he would only lob order after order at her, insisting that she return to the castle at once.

Bree would do no such thing. As much as she hated to upset him, losing him to whatever the Wilde Fae had planned was far worse than that. If Eurig and Bree did not work fast, the curse might be the least of their worries. Lives were in danger. Lives of those she cared about. And Bree would do anything to save the ones she loved.

In the corner of the room, Bree spotted another dead raven. She furrowed her eyebrows, and she glanced around to see if any others could be found within this room. But only silence answered her. Eurig had already removed the villagers who had fallen in the pub, so there was no one left in here but Bree. Bree and the raven.

Curiosity nibbled at her brain, and she pushed her stool back against the stone ground. It groaned underneath her, the wood creaking as it shuddered across the floor. She hopped down and crossed the room, kneeling down beside the blood-soaked raven.

She cocked her head and stared at it. If it weren't for the blood, and there was lots of it, she might believe the raven had fallen prey to the curse as well. The horses hadn't succumbed, but that did not mean every animal would resist it. Unfortunately, this raven's fate had ripped it from this world. Something sharp had sliced through it stomach, a wound that had caused it to bleed out on the floor.

But why? What did it have to do with the curse?

Bree took one glance over her shoulder at the open door that led out into the village square. And then she glanced at the bird, reaching out with timid fingers. She placed one hand gently against the dark feathers, stiffening at the warmth she felt from the bird. Bree's heart began to hammer hard in her chest, and a strange sickly sensation churned through her gut.

She swallowed hard, and then pressed her hand even harder against the raven. "What happened to you?"

Bree listened, even knowing that she would never get an answer. Her fingertips buzzed, electricity lighting up every inch of her skin. With a gasp, Bree snapped her hand back and stared down at the bird. She had felt that sensation before, but only once. And it was a sensation she would never forget, no matter how many years she might live on this earth.

It was the very same sensation she'd felt when she used Taveon's powers to heal Rafe's wound. But that was impossible. She had to be imagining things. For one, she was not even in communication with Taveon at the moment. The walls were firmly up between them. When she had healed Rafe, she had only done so with Taveon's help. He had sent his power into her body. She hadn't claimed it herself.

And two, well...the bird was dead. How could she heal something that was not even alive?

Still, there was no denying what she had felt. That bright sparking electricity that filled her soul, making her feel full of the most glorious light imaginable. With a shuddering breath, Bree reached out once again and placed her trembling hands against the raven's blood-soaked feathers. It was still and stiff, though it was warm, as though it had only died moments ago. She focused on its tiny body, closing her eyes to breathe in its aura.

Underneath her fingertips, she swore she felt its body twitch. She gritted her teeth, her entire body filling with Taveon's healing powers. It was a storm in her veins, churning through her at an impossible speed. Her breath shuddered from her lungs, and her entire body felt as though it was consumed by flames.

And then she pushed every single bit of that power down to her hands, to the tips of her fingers, and into the poor creature who had died for this curse. The magic stormed out of her in a rush, leaving her to gasp for air as if she hadn't breathed in a million years. Her whole body went weak, and black creeped in the edges of her vision. In the distance, she could feel Taveon pounding against the wall she had erected between them. Even with those walls there, he knew what she was doing. No doubt he'd felt her suck his healing power right from his veins.

With a deep breath, Bree cracked open her eyes. The tiny raven still lay on the ground, and a rush of disappointment burned through Bree's heart. It had been ridiculous to think that she could have healed a dead animal, but she had truly hoped she could. Tears even pricked the corners of her eyes as she gazed at the horrible blood that had soaked into the floorboards. The raven's blood. The poor creature would never again soar through the skies.

And then its tiny wing twitched, so lightly that she couldn't be certain it had even happened. She held her breath tight in her throat as she stared down at the creature. The wing twitched again. A single eye cracked open. Its beak parted. Bree sucked in a sharp breath and jumped to her feet, stumbling away from the now living bird.

Because yes, it was alive. Very much alive. So alive that its little wings beat faster, and it lifted its body from the floor. Bree stared at the creature with an open mouth, her heart racing like a horse in her chest. She swore the raven looked at her and gazed deep within her soul, seeing the truth of what she had done.

Footsteps pounded on the wooden floor, and Bree jerked her head toward the sound. It was Eurig. He was staring at the raven with an ashen face and eyes so wide they could rival the moon.

"Is that the same raven we found?" His voice was

rough and ragged, as if he'd run twenty miles without pausing for breath.

"Not the same one," Bree said slowly. "But it was like the others. It was dead only a few moments ago."

"Dead?" Eurig took a timid step further into the pub, his gaze locked on the raven that now fluttered before them both. The creature was not only alive, but it did not even appear to be wounded anymore. "But how is that even possible? Are you certain it was dead? And not just cursed?"

"Trust me, it was dead. Its stomach had been sliced open, and the blood all over the floor was the bird's." Bree swallowed hard, more than a little bit nervous to tell Eurig exactly what she was capable of now. "I...healed it."

Eurig's eyes widened. "You can't be serious. No one can bring the dead back to life."

"Well, it appears Taveon can." Bree lifted her eyebrows, hoping that Eurig would follow her train of thought so that she did not have to explain how exactly she'd come to enjoy this strange, unsettling power.

"You can heal others because of your bond, can't you?" Eurig asked, nodding. "I thought so. When my sword went deeper into Rafferty than I intended...well, I am glad I was right." He shook his head, frowning. "But being able to heal is a hell of a lot different than being able to breathe life back into a dead creature. I do not know if this is a good thing,

Bree. I do not know if that is a kind of power anyone should be able to wield."

Bree knew he was right, in a way, but she did not want to admit it. She had never wanted her beastly powers, or the power to shapeshift into *any* animal at all. She had never even particularly wanted the enhanced senses that many fae possessed, such as better hearing, sight, or smell. She wanted something more. Something powerful. Something that could truly make a difference.

And this was it. The power to bring the dead back to life.

Bree was eager to head straight into the lands of the Wilde Fae, her intense need to save both Rafe and Taveon overwhelming the logic in her mind. Eurig understood. He was no stranger to torment or the realization that you would do anything to save the ones you loved. But Eurig was not about to let Bree rush into a dangerous situation half-cocked either.

It was far too late to be trekking through the forest at this hour. The two of them had endured attacks already, and if they wanted to beat the Wilde Fae, they would be much better off resting instead of rushing through a bloodied forest once again. So, Eurig insisted they stay in the village for the night. He had moved all of the villagers into their beds earlier in the day, but there were still a handful of open ones they were able to use to rest for the night.

The beds were in the same cottage, though in different rooms of the house. To Eurig, it felt like Bree was miles away instead of only feet from where he lay. With a groan, he rolled over on the hard mattress to stare up at the wooden ceiling. He wanted nothing more than to go to her. He had seen the way she'd looked into his eyes the day before in the forest clearing when they'd been healing each other's wounds. There had been something in her expression, something he had never seen before.

And it had scared the hell out of him.

He couldn't help but be drawn to her, but he knew it was wrong. For one, he knew she was spoken for. Either by Rafe or by Taveon, he wasn't sure. They definitely both loved her, and her actions made it clear that she loved them, too. There was no room for Eurig in the equation, no matter how beautiful she looked when the moonlight caressed her skin.

The floorboards creaked, and he shifted toward the door to find Bree hovering just inside of his room. She had found a loose tunic in the wardrobe, one that barely hit the top of her thighs. Eurig swallowed hard and tried to avert his gaze, but he couldn't help but drink in the sight of her smooth skin.

"Can you not sleep?" Eurig asked, his voice rough with an emotion he could not let her see.

She toed the wooden floor with her bare feet. "Not really. It's kind of hard to relax knowing what tomorrow brings. We have to infiltrate the Wilde Fae. The fate of the Court and everyone I care about depends on what happens when we do. If we fail..."

"We won't fail. I will not allow it." Years ago, Eurig had vowed to do whatever he could for Taveon. It was why he'd come to the castle in the first place, and it was why he'd stayed even after discovering the training he would be forced to do. And it was what had driven him to seek answers beyond the castle, to find a way to bring his old friend out of his slumber. But it was not his only reason anymore. Eurig felt driven by something more, and that something more was standing right in front of him.

"Yeah, but it looks like you can't sleep either." Bree took a timid step toward him, but she averted her gaze, as if she couldn't bear to look at him. "If you're not worried, then what is it?"

"Oh, I worry about a lot of things." Eurig pushed up from the bed and settled his feet on the floor. "I worry about that dead raven. I worry what will happen to Taveon if we are wrong. And I worry about you. Don't think I can't see how much this is tearing you apart."

"You worry about...me?" Eurig swore that Bree's cheeks flushed with color.

"Of course I do," he said. "I can see how much you care about them both."

"Them both?" Bree asked, her face screwing up in confusion. "Who do you mean?"

Eurig stood and took one slow step toward Bree, as if his body was moving out of its own volition. "Rafferty. Taveon. Who else would I be talking about?"

Bree's eyes widened, and she nodded. "You could have meant Taveon, Rafe, or Dagen. Or anyone else who calls the castle home. I do care about them all, you know."

Lord Dagen. Did he hold a piece of Bree's heart as well?

"When you say that you care about them…" Eurig stopped himself, and he took a step back. The direction of this conversation needed to change. Her answer did not matter. He knew the truth. She belonged to one of them and not to him. And even if she did not, Bree deserved far more than a bastard outcast from a little plank above the sea."

Bree's entire face was the color of blood, and she stammered when she finally replied. "Are you asking me what I think you're asking?"

"No," he said, turning slightly away and clenching his jaw.

"Yes, you are," Bree said. "I can tell what you're doing. You're trying to pretend that you don't want to know the answer to your question, but I can tell that you *do* want to hear it. So, I'm going to tell you."

Eurig's gut clenched tight. "Bree, don't."

"It's true. Rafe and I are in some sort of…relationship. A romantic one." Bree sucked in a deep breath.

"As for the others, Lord Dagen and King Taveon, we share something special, but I can't explain it. And I know they care about me, too."

"So, you are a taken female. You have been spoken for." He hated the words, even though they were true. No, *especially* because they were true.

"I don't know what I am. But I do know that I care about more than one male alone, and as confusing as it is, I refuse to believe there is anything wrong with it." Bree sucked in a deep breath, and she stepped up before Eurig, tucking her finger underneath his chin and forcing him to meet her eyes. "And when I say that I care about more than one, that includes you."

CHAPTER 22
BREE

Bree's heart was racing so fast that she could barely hear Eurig's words over the sound of it echoing in her ears. She didn't know what had gotten into her. First, she'd tiptoed into his room, hoping he would be awake. And then she had braved forward, telling him exactly how she felt. He would probably turn her away now, even though he had been the one to ask the question.

If he wanted to know if she was taken, then surely that must mean he cared, right?

"Bree," Eurig breathed, his entire body tense underneath the small touch of her finger on his chin. "I could never wrong Taveon like that."

"It would not be wronging Taveon," Bree insisted. "He's more than well enough aware of my feelings for Rafe, and Rafe's feelings for me. It doesn't bother him. Trust me, I would know."

"This is crazy," Eurig said, but he did not take a step away from her.

"And why is it so crazy?" Bree asked.

"Have you ever heard of such a thing? Sharing a female? It just is not done."

"Well, there you are wrong," Bree said, her mind flicking back to the things she'd been dwelling on these past few months. "In the Light Fae realm, Greater Fae females have more than one mate all the time."

Okay, so that was an exaggeration. It happened, but not all the time. Still, it was evidence that what she was suggesting wasn't as crazy as Eurig thought. But even if it was, nothing in the world had ever felt more right. She cared for more than one male, and more than one cared for her, and she wouldn't want it any other way.

Eurig raised an eyebrow. "Multiple mates?"

Bree nodded, holding her breath and hoping that he wouldn't find the idea as foreign as she feared. "That's right. One female. Many males."

"Many?" Eurig pursed his lips, lips that Bree was desperate to kiss. "How many?"

"Norah, the new Queen of the Light Fae, has four." Bree's heart thumped. And *she* wanted four. Rafferty, Taveon, Dagen, and now...Eurig. Four Dark Fae males to call her own. They were all so different, yet they all owned a piece of her heart.

"Hmm." Eurig leaned closer, dropping his fore-head to hers. "And the mates...they do not mind this?"

Bree knew that Eurig was not asking about Norah's mates, though he hadn't specified. He was asking about hers. "Norah's mates understand that she loves them all. And that they love her."

There was so much still left unspoken between Bree and Rafe and Taveon, and even Dagen. But she knew they understood her feelings were spread further than toward one single male. Through the bond, Taveon was silent, but Bree knew he was there, watching and listening to her conversation with Eurig. And she knew that he could read the truth in her heart and feel the affection that had been building inside of her.

He did not object, and he wouldn't.

Eurig gazed into her eyes as if searching for the truth. For a moment, she thought he would pull away from her once again and deny her the intimacy she yearned from him. But then his lips were on hers, his kiss rough and fast. She clutched his tunic, and her body arched toward him.

With a grunt, he pulled her on top of his chest so that she was straddling his hips. Between her thighs, she could feel the hard length of him pressing against her core. A delicious thrill shot through her gut, causing a flame to spark to life.

Her core burned with need as Eurig's kiss deep-ened. The scent of him was overwhelming, and she swore she heard the crash of waves on a distant shore. His hand found her hips, squeezing tight as he pulled her harder against his cock.

By the forest, she wanted him. All of him.

Bree pulled back, her breath ragged. She gazed down at him, a new spark of heat bursting forth at the delicious look in his eye. He licked his lips and curled his finger, motioning for her to come back in for another kiss.

"I want you inside of me," she breathed, face flushing.

It wasn't like Bree to be so forward, but her outposter was bringing a new side of her out in full force.

Eurig's lips twisted into a wicked smile. He wrapped his arms around her body and flipped her onto the bed. His hands found her tunic, and he'd ripped it in half before she even knew what was happening. Seconds later, he was just as naked as she was.

She'd seen him naked many times by now but never like this. Never so...aroused. Her core pulsed, and a wetness coated her thighs. That wicked smile still donning his lips, Eurig flipped Bree onto her stomach and lifted her hips into the air so that the entire back of her was exposed to his hungry eyes.

He leaned forward, dropping his head to hers so that he could whisper into her ear. His hot breath tickled her skin, making her entire body dissolve into a trembling mess. "Are you ready for me, Bree?"

She swallowed hard, practically panting with the need for him. "Please."

Eurig rubbed his hands across her bare ass and then squeezed her thighs tight. The length of him pressed against her, and he moaned when he felt the wetness between her thighs. With a low growl, he pushed inside of her. Sparks lit up in Bree's eyes. She shuddered as he pushed in, deeper and deeper until he hit the very back of her core.

She let out a moan of pleasure and need. Her body clenched around him, and a desperate desire made her rock back against his cock.

"Bree," he growled, his fingers digging hard into her hips. "How do you feel so damn good?"

Bree smiled and rocked against him again, taking pleasure in the pure, unadulterated pleasure that shook through Eurig's body. It made her feel strong and powerful, making her male experience the kind of bliss that caused his entire body to shake from the force of it.

And then he rocked against her in turn, his hardness hitting the back of her core once again. She cried out, a new wave of stars dotting her eyes. Deep, deep pleasure began to build inside of her, sending her body so close to the edge of endless waves of relief.

But she did not want it to stop. Not yet. Not now.

She wanted this moment with Eurig to stretch on for endless hours. Days. Weeks. Months.

Eurig slammed into her once again, the pace of his thrusts quickening with each passing beat. He shuddered against her, and her body pulsed around his cock. All logical thought fled from her mind as the pleasure of his body consumed her. Nothing else existed but the heat between her thighs.

Another thrust. Another moan. Bree's breaths grew ragged. Eurig thrusted his hardness even deeper between her thighs. And then she was gone. Pleasure exploded through her core, her entire body pulsing from the release that poured from within her. Eurig cried out only seconds behind her, emptying his seed into her trembling body.

They stayed there like that until their heartbeats slowed and their breathing became steady. And then Eurig pulled Bree to his chest before lowering them back down onto the hard mattress. She rested her head in the crook of his shoulder and ran her fingers along the hard panes of his stomach. Her heart felt full, her body felt weak, and all the fear and pain she'd felt the past few days had disappeared into a puff of smoke.

"That was nice," Bree whispered into his chest.

He caressed her shoulder, twisting his head to drop a soft kiss on her forehead. "It was more than nice. I have been thinking about how you would feel for awhile now, Bree. Imagine my surprise when it was far better than anything I could have imagined."

A thrill went through her heart, and suddenly, she felt very shy. "Right back at you. You felt better than I imagined, I mean."

"I only wish our coupling could have the happy ending you want, Bree," Eurig said sadly.

Frowning, she sat up on her elbow and gazed down at him. "Why wouldn't it?"

"We are on a dangerous mission, one fraught with violence." Eurig sighed and pulled her back to his chest. "I worry what will happen if we are unable to save the Court. If the Wilde Fae invade the castle...we could end up as prisoners. Or worse."

"Or we could win," Bree said, a new determination shooting through her gut. They would get through this. Not only for the others but for each other, too. "Don't give up hope, Eurig. We're a good team, don't forget."

A lazy smile spread across his face. "That we are."

"Besides," she said, half-teasing, half-serious, "you're one of my mates now. That means you're stuck with me for awhile."

Eurig met Bree's grin with one of his own. "I wouldn't have it any other way."

CHAPTER 23
BREE

The next morning, Bree almost hated to leave behind the tiny village. Their short time spent there had been so peaceful, minus the whole dead raven thing. But there was no time to spare. They needed to get through the entire forest if they wanted to make the journey before the next setting of the moon. And then they would head straight to the nearest Wilde Fae clan, hoping to find a way to reverse the curse before it was too late.

As much as Bree hated to take from these fae, she went through a couple of the pantries to collect some supplies for the coming journey. She stuffed a few packets of dried fruits into her rucksack, not bothering to look over her shoulder when she heard Eurig's footsteps behind her.

"Who are you and what are you doing in here?" An icy voice rang out behind her.

Bree jumped to her feet and whirled toward the voice, her heart raging hard when she saw who stood before her. It was the female from the pub, the one they had found face down on the floor. Bree shook her head and stepped back, her legs slamming into the wall. How was this possible? Only hours ago, she'd been dead to the world.

"I…" For once, Bree was speechless.

"We're travelers," Eurig said, standing on the steps just outside of the house and calling through the open door. "When we arrived here last night, everyone was in a trance. We thought you were under some kind of curse."

The female's eyes flicked toward Eurig and then back to Bree, suspicion churning in her irises. "Aye. One minute, I was having my nightly drink. The next, I felt like I was in a tunnel. I couldn't see or hear a damn thing but I was awake all the same. And then what do you know, the next thing I know I'm coming to in my bed. At first, I thought maybe I'd just been too drunk, but then here you two are."

Bree nodded. That sounded exactly like what had happened to Taveon. This female had been cursed, the same as everyone else in the Court. But she was awake now. And if she was awake…

Excitement rippled through Bree, and she threw down the walls she kept between her and Taveon. She called out through the bond, anticipation rippling through her veins. If this female was back to normal, then maybe that meant Taveon would be, too. She had no idea how or why, but that wasn't what was important, not when she would finally be able to look into his eyes once again.

"Taveon?" Bree said, unable to keep the excitement out of her voice. "The curse, has it been lifted?"

A moment passed in silence, but then he was there in all of his Taveon-like glory. There was no excitement on his end though. He felt the same as he always did, a kaleidoscope of dark, churning emotions.

"I am afraid that nothing has changed here, at least not that I am aware of." His words made her stomach drop. "Why? Please tell me you have not stormed the Wilde Fae."

Of course he would not know that she hadn't left the village yet. She had tried so hard to keep this morning's actions hidden from him, knowing that he would try to talk her out of it. And grill her about what she had done to the raven.

"Not yet," she said, trying to keep the disappointment out of her voice. "We just...well, we met a female here. She was cursed and now she isn't. I thought that maybe..."

She wasn't sure how much more she should say. As much as she wanted to give him hope, she did not wish to give him false information that turned out to lead nowhere.

"Come back, Bree," Taveon said, not even referencing the revelation she'd just had. "I know you are trying to hide your emotions from me, but I can feel hints of them all the same. You're upset. You're full of anger. You want revenge. It will make you act recklessly, like you did with that raven. You do not understand the power you have used, power you never should have accessed."

Bree's eyes fluttered shut, and she fought back the urge to turn her voice harsh against him. "Maybe if you told me exactly where your power comes from, then I would have a better understanding of the power I'm accessing. Until then..." She hated to do it, but she had no other choice. Bree was going to infiltrate the Wilde Fae, because she would do what she had to do in order to get Taveon back.

They traveled all day in their beastly forms, and they made it out of the forest just in time to see the last silver streaks of the moon against the night sky. Their horses stood waiting for them on the dirt path, stomping their hooves aimlessly against the ground. Eurig and Bree swapped a look, one that said far more than words ever would. Together, they were seeing strange things about this realm that had felt hidden before now.

"To be on the safe side, we should camp out again for the night," Eurig said as he gave his golden horse an affectionate stroke. The horse neighed and shook its mane, communicating exactly the same emotion Bree felt.

"Yeah, no. That is a terrible idea. The last time we camped out here, one of those Hawkborn maniacs attacked us and almost killed me. Or at least came as close to killing me as it could." Bree gave her own horse an affectionate pat on the head and leaned against it, breathing in the musty scent of earth. "Besides, there's no telling how long the Wilde Fae will wait to launch their attack on the undefended castle. We really don't have any time to waste, Eurig. We need to get to them before anything else happens."

Bree didn't mention the fae who had awoken in the village. One by one, they'd all risen from their curse. Every time another fae had stood on his feet, Bree couldn't help but check in on Taveon, her hope growing with every single beat of her heart. But still, he remained as he was, stuck inside of his own head in the darkness. She didn't understand why the villagers were coming out of it, but Taveon was still stuck in his form.

Perhaps it was because the Wilde Fae had not attacked the castle as of yet. They'd ransacked the village and had gotten what they wanted, and now they were heading on to the next. She couldn't think of any other explanation for what had happened, which meant Bree might still have time to stop the Wilde Fae from finishing what they had started.

Without another word, Eurig and Bree mounted their horses and started down the dirt path that would lead to the Wilde Fae lands. Once again, Bree was forced to put her trust in the outposter. She had no idea what part of this realm the Wilde Fae called home. She knew they lived in clans, scattered throughout the rolling hills and the forests of Underworld, but that information was about as vague as one could get.

"What exactly is your plan here, Bree?" Eurig asked, raising his voice to be heard over the pounding hooves on the dirt path.

"Simple. I will sneak in, find their leader, wait until they have an interesting conversation, and listen in to whatever they have to say." Bree gripped the reins tighter in her hands, knowing exactly how ridiculous the entire thing sounded. "I figure if they have some sort of plan to attack the castle, then the ruler will need to talk to his underlings about it at some point. As soon as we know what they plan to do, we can figure out the best way to stop them."

Eurig let out a chuckle. It started as a soft sound, so low that Bree could barely hear it. But then it grew louder, so loud that it became a booming sound across the rolling hills. Irritation flickered through Bree, and she shot him a sharp look. She knew her plan sounded a little weird, but it wasn't *that* ridiculous. Hell, she had done far more ridiculous things since she'd come to Underworld.

"Let me get this straight," Eurig said. "You plan to lurk around in the Wilde Fae's territory for a long length of time, and you expect that they would have no idea you were in their midst." Eurig raised an eyebrow and shook his head. "Taveon really does need to up your book learning. You won't last longer than five minutes in there without them hearing you or smelling you. Their senses are far more enhanced than you give them credit for."

Shit. Bree didn't want to admit it to Eurig, but she'd totally forgotten all about the whole enhanced senses thing. That put more than a little bit of a damper on her plans. Because Eurig was right. Bree's entire plan hinged on one thing, and that was her ability to sneak around for an indefinite amount of time undetected.

No matter. She would just have to be more careful. Her footsteps would be quiet, and she would mask her scent as best she could.

Halfway to the territory, Bree spotted a swamp. She pointed it out to Eurig and asked him to stop. After she jumped down from her horse, she strode straight toward the swamp and dunked down inside. The water was freezing, and the murky depths stank of death and decay, but it would do.

When she joined Eurig back at the horses, the look on his face was not one she had expected. He shook his head and laughed some more. "Do you have any idea how ridiculous you look?"

"Laugh it up," she said with a smug smile. "But this will prevent the Wilde Fae from smelling me. They'll have no idea a shape-shifting fae is in their midst when every hint of me is doused out by the swamp water."

He raised his eyebrows, still laughing. "You do realize that the smell of that swamp water is far more potent than your own body odor? They will smell you a mile away."

Bree's cheeks flushed with heat, but thankfully, he wouldn't be able to see it this time, not with the mud caking her face. "The point is, I just smell like the earth. When they catch this scent, they're not going to think that it's someone lurking nearby."

"If you say so." Eurig's smile never faltered as he watched Bree try to mount her horse once again. This was one thing she hadn't thought through. Her legs were coated with the mud, making her skin slippery against the horse's back. Every time she thought she'd made it on, she ended up tumbling over the other side and falling face first on the dirt.

After at least a dozen attempts, Eurig broke free of his saddle and jumped down to help her clamber onto her horse. Even with his help, Bree barely managed to get a grasp on the reins. She slid one way and then another, the mud from her skin slipping against his. Just as she was about to take another hard tumble to the ground, Eurig caught her against his chest.

Her face smashed against him, and her heart tripped.

"Careful," he said with a chuckle. "Or you'll end up falling right back into my bed again."

Bree's entire body warmed at the thought of it. It was the first time he had brought up their night together since they had awoken. And it was the first time she'd let herself dwell on the memories of his arms wrapped tight around her body as she moaned in pleasure.

Swallowing hard, she stared deep into his golden eyes, wanting nothing more than to give in to the desire twisting in her core. But she couldn't. Not right now. The Court was depending on her. Swamp water or not, it was time to infiltrate the enemy.

CHAPTER 24
BREE

When they reached the nearest territory of the Wilde Fae, nothing was as Bree expected. She had conjured up images in her head of vicious creatures building forts within the very depths of the earth. Instead, the rolling hills were covered in rows upon rows of cute little huts, made from grass and the limbs of the nearby forest. There was no chaos here or violence. Instead, Bree found nothing but peaceful silence.

Eurig frowned and jumped down from his horse. "Something is wrong. It is far too quiet here."

"It is the middle of the night," Bree said in a whisper. "Can they all be sleeping?"

Eurig jerked his head. "The Wilde Fae enjoy the night, reveling in the deepest parts of darkness. They celebrate it. On a normal night, this place would be an orgy of drinking, dancing, and..." Eurig swallowed hard and glanced away. "And sex."

Bree's entire body warmed, and she was far too aware of what she must look like right now, covered in the mud from the swamp. Why, oh why, had she thought that was a good idea? He probably thought she looked like a drowned rat.

"So, then what do you think is going on?" Bree asked, turning the conversation back onto the task at hand. She could not think of Eurig right now, not like that, though it was impossible to rid her mind of memories of the feel of his skin against hers.

"Either they are not here, or..." Eurig let the rest of his sentence fall into silence as he tied his horse to the nearest tree and turned toward the Wilde Fae camp. Bree followed just behind him, grabbing a dagger from her rucksack just in case.

They slowly eased their way down the hill, careful to keep themselves hidden in the shadows just in case a Wilde Fae was keeping watch from somewhere hidden from their own prying eyes. Bree could barely breathe as they stepped into the middle of the huts, and her heartbeat was racing so fast that her entire body trembled from the force of it.

Eurig stepped up close to the door of the nearest hut, ducking his head low so that he could gaze inside. She reached out toward him, instinctively, desperately wanting to pull him back close in fear that a Wilde Fae would catch him lurking around their hut. Eurig's back stiffened and he sucked in a sharp breath, causing Bree's heart to throttle into the next gear.

She expected a hand to reach out from the depths of the hut and wrap itself around Eurig's throat, but instead, nothing happened. Eurig stumbled back from the hut and whirled toward Bree with wide eyes.

"What is it?" Bree asked. "What's happened?"

"They're all dead. That, or cursed." Eurig sighed and ran a hand down his tired face. "I would put bets on them being cursed."

Bree's eyes widened, and she shook her head from side to side in disbelief. "That's impossible. They can't be cursed. Not if they're the ones who were doing the cursing."

"You're right," Eurig said with a frown. "The only way these Wilde Fae could be cursed is if they weren't the ones behind it in the first place."

All the blood drained from Bree's face, not because of worry for these fae but because of what that meant. If they were not the ones who had cast the curse on Taveon and the rest of the Court, then who was? The truth was, Bree and Eurig had no other leads other than what they had found in the fae village. She had staked all of her hope on the Wilde Fae. And now that they had discovered they were wrong, Bree felt as though all the fight had gone out of her in the single blink of an eye.

"There's more," Eurig said, his voice edged in something akin to wariness. He eyed Bree with a strange expression, one that made her feel as if he did not want to share whatever else he had just seen inside that hut.

"Tell me, Eurig," Bree said. "It's only fair that I know."

"Only if you promise that you will do nothing about it. And I do mean nothing."

What the hell did that mean? And why did he look as though he almost feared her in a way? Bree sighed, shook her head, and shoved past Eurig. He might be built like a tank, but he hadn't expected her to charge straight past him so that she could see whatever it was that he had discovered in the hut.

Inside, she saw three fallen Wilde Fae, their signature yellow skin pale from the lack of light in their eyes. All around them, dead ravens dotted the floor, and their blood was a painting against the beige surfaces of the hut. Bree jerked back, shaking her head. More dead ravens. Everywhere they turned, there were more.

They had been in the castle, they had been in the village, and now they were here. They were always wherever the curse was found.

Pieces of the puzzle began to fit together in Bree's mind. Dead ravens, the curse. It was all connected. Including what had happened to the fae in the village. Bree's eyes widened, and her heart began to jerk inside her chest. She whirled toward Eurig, and his face reflected every thought raging through her mind.

"That's why they came back," Bree whispered. "Because of the raven. It was dead, but I brought it back. And then the next morning, the fae came back, too."

Eurig held up his hands as if in warning or surrender. Or both. "Bree. Let's not jump to conclusions. I know it seems that way, but those two events might not be connected at all."

She shook her head and took a step away from him. "You've suspected it all this time, haven't you? You don't seem surprised at all. You came to this conclusion back in the village, didn't you?"

"The thought occurred to me, but it's nothing more than a hunch that is probably wrong," Eurig said slowly. "Just because it happened once does not mean it would happen again. In fact, it is more likely to have no effect at all."

"But there is a chance that it *did* make every difference in the world," Bree said in a whisper. "There is a chance that if I bring these ravens back to life that every single Wilde Fae who has fallen here will wake up. And if that's the case, then you know what I need to do. This is how we bring Rafe and Taveon back."

"That power is not normal, Bree," Eurig said, his voice strained. "Now is not the time to jump to conclusions. Please. We have found what we came here to find. I think it is time for us to go back to the castle now."

Bree shook her head and took one more step away from him. He knew just as well as she did that she wasn't going anywhere until she healed one of the ravens in this place. She had to know if this was the cure, if this was the way to bring her males back into the land of the living.

Bree ducked through the door of the hut and placed her hand upon the raven's feathers before Eurig could stop her. The first time she'd tried to cast Taveon's power, it had taken time for her to wrap her mind around it. It had been foreign, and it had been unknown to her. But now it felt like home, and it came to her in a rush without even the slightest request from her mind. As if it knew exactly what she needed it to do.

Sparks filled her body with that brilliant light that almost blinded her soul. Her entire body felt consumed by fire, flames licking every inch of her skin. Bree's heart burned, and tears stung her eyes. Behind her, she could hear Eurig roaring in the distance, but she blocked out the sound. The only thing that mattered now was the bird. The tiny little raven's life. Because its very soul might lead to the only cure they had.

Bree poured the healing light into the twisted wings, gritting her teeth against the force of it. When she finally opened her eyes, she stared down at the creature. As before, it slowly twitched, every moment bringing with it more movement.

Eurig's breath was ragged as he stood just behind her, gazing down at the creature with a tortured expression on his face. "Bree. What have you done? I told you not to do anything rash."

"You don't make my decisions for me, I'm afraid," Bree said, as gently as she could. She knew he was only trying to keep her safe. He was trying to do what was best for her. But only Bree could be the one to make her own decisions. Not Eurig. Not Rafe. Not even Taveon, who was pounding against the walls with as much anguish as Eurig displayed on his face.

The raven lifted into the air, took one long look at Bree, and then it was off through the open door of the hut to join his brethren in the night sky. Bree felt her heart lift at the sight. That was two now. Two lives that had been lost, now brought back into the realm of the living.

Eurig and Bree found some chairs and made camp just outside the hut where Bree had healed the raven. It had taken several hours for the villagers to wake up from their curse after Bree had healed the raven there. It would likely take several more hours again.

It was hard to stay still. Bree was itching to get back to the Court. Now that they had learned the Wilde Fae were not behind this—not this Clan of

Wilde Fae at least—she was desperate to return to the castle and ensure that the true attackers had not descended on those stone walls.

It was funny. King Midas had built his hulking monstrosity so carefully all those years ago, demonstrating his power, his cruelty, and his cunning. He'd designed the structures in such a way that it would be next to impossible for an invading army to reach the Keep.

He hadn't considered this curse though. That changed everything.

After what felt like years, the Wilde Fae began to wake up. Eurig and Bree stayed just long enough to see them stirring, slowly standing with confusion wrinkling their skin. But they didn't want to stick around much longer than that. Yes, they had managed to undo the curse on them, but the Wilde Fae were nothing like the villagers. They were dangerous, cruel, and chaotic. And they were far more likely to stab Bree on the spot than to hear her out.

Eurig was quiet as they rode down the dirt path that would lead them back to the castle, but he didn't need to speak for Bree to know exactly what he was thinking. He did not approve of what she'd done, and he didn't want her to do it again, even knowing that it would likely bring every fae inside that castle back.

"You know I have to do it," Bree finally said, her

entire heart lifting when she spotted the first peak of the highest tower on the distant horizon.

"I know," Eurig said with a heavy sigh, glancing over from where he clung tightly to his horse's reins. "But before you do, promise me one thing."

Bree arched an eyebrow. "What's that?"

"Ask Taveon to tell you what he is," Eurig said, his voice firm and strong.

Bree opened her mouth to reply, but she didn't have a chance to speak. A single arrow slammed into the ground just in front of her, and her horse jerked to a sudden stop, neighing as it kicked its front legs high in the air.

Bree barely held on to the reins as the horse bucked underneath her.

And then a storm of arrows rained down.

Bree's heart galloped in her chest as she twisted on the horse to see where the attackers were hiding. Another dozen arrows soared through the air. Bree kicked the horse's sides and yelled, flicking the reins as it bolted forward. Eurig did the same, the two of them racing toward the front gates that were still too far in the distance to see.

"What do we do, Eurig?" Bree shouted into the chilly air that bit her face.

He frowned as he turned to look behind them. Despite the intensity of the situation, she couldn't help but gape at him. He was not even holding on to the reins as his entire body curved toward the attackers now riding after them, dozens of horses kicking dust into the night air. Eurig's leg muscles rippled as he rode, and his golden eyes glinted underneath the light of the moon.

She had never seen anything more powerful.

The riders behind them began to gain ground, and Eurig motioned for Bree to...

Jump. He wanted her to jump off her horse. Bree shook her head, refusing to do any such thing. Not only would that hurt like hell, but they'd be stuck on the ground where the rangers would no doubt hit them with their constant lobby of arrows.

"Trust me," he mouthed.

Their eyes locked, and something passed between them. Affection, heat, and a kind of trust that she didn't feel she could ever earn. Not from him. Not from anyone.

Eurig pushed off his horse and tumbled to the ground. Gritting her teeth, Bree followed suit. Her body slammed hard on the dirt, and her shoulder screamed in pain. Eurig was beside her within an instant, grabbing her arm and hauling her to her feet.

He pressed his forehead against hers and hissed, "Shift. Change into your beast. It's the only way we'll be fast enough to beat them to the castle."

Shift. Of course. Because Eurig was right. In her beastly form, Bree was far faster than any horse, any human, or even any fae. She took one glance behind her at the riders quickly approaching and forced her mind to center on what she had to do. Eurig had already begun to change, his lion coming to him far easier than Bree could claim her wolf.

And there was no time to waste.

Bree's arms and legs stretched out into long powerful limbs as she succumbed to the power of her beast. Claws ripped out through her fingertips, and her head shifted and shook as sharp teeth cut through her jaw. Her entire body ached from the force of such a quick shift, but she did not pause to catch her breath. The distant sound of hooves on dirt had grown louder and louder, signaling that their attackers were only feet behind them.

Beside her, she could hear the panting of Eurig's lion, and then his roar that shook out across the rolling hillside. He took off in a run, and the beast within her yearned to follow. Together, they raced across the dirt, the night blurring by in silver streaks.

The sound of hooves grew fainter as the massive gates of the castle rose up before them. They reached the iron entrance within moments, and somehow, Eurig had transformed back into his fae self just as he slowed to a stop before them. He reached up and pushed open the gates, and the iron clanged from the force of his touch. Bree galloped just behind him, her beast making claim to her body. As much as she had practiced shifting these past few months, she had not mastered it, not fully and completely as Eurig had. She would need time to catch her breath before she could shift back into her mortal self.

But that didn't matter. They had made it. Eurig slammed the gates behind them, blocking out the riders and their arrows. For now.

୧♾୨

After Bree had shifted back into her fae form, they headed straight to her quarters where she threw on another set of fighting leathers. She tried not to think about the torn shreds of her Light Fae leathers that she had been forced to leave behind on the dirt path. She had managed to grab her dagger in time, but there was no way to gather the scraps of her clothes. Those fighting leathers had been her only link to her past, the only reminder of who she truly was. And now they were gone.

"Who were they?" Bree asked as she shoved a tunic over her head, blinking the tears out of her eyes. "Another Wilde Fae clan?"

The truth was, she hadn't caught a particularly good look at their attackers. She had been far too focused on shifting and charging toward the castle gates. But she had caught a glimpse of their faces, and she had seen the size of their forms. They didn't look like Wilde Fae, or at least any of the full-blooded Wilde Fae that she had seen in the past. Those fae had been massive, their skin tinged with green or yellow. And their faces had been twisted and gnarled. The fae she had seen on the horses chasing them…well, they had looked just like any of the other fae at Court.

Eurig's jaw rippled as he clenched his teeth together. "As hard as it is for me to believe this, I am afraid those were outposters you saw. I recognized some of them. Friends of mine from way back then. And they recognized me, too."

Bree froze, and her gut churned with dread. "Outposters? Are you certain?"

Eurig gave a solemn nod. "I am more certain of that than I am of anything else. I want to be surprised by this, but it makes sense. The Queen has likely decided to make her move against the Court here. The outposters have been unhappy for years, and the Queen's wrath has only increased as the years have gone by. She did not trust Midas, though she did fear him, so it makes sense that she would choose Taveon's coronation as her chance to attack and take the throne. I would not put it past her. She has already taken one crown."

"But I thought there was a truce," Bree said in a whisper. There had been dozens of riders chasing them, and if Eurig was right, there would be far more than that when they decided to attack the castle. He had said there were thousands of outposters. Thousands upon thousands. And they were more highly-trained than anyone thought. Eurig was the perfect example of that.

"There was a truce between King Clarke and King

Midas. Both of them are now dead," Eurig said in a hard voice.

Bree fought back the urge to sit down. This was bad. Really bad. She needed to find that raven and bring it back to life, and she just had to hope that the Court would wake up before the Queen launched her army at the gates. As strong as the barriers were, and as much of an advantage as the castle held against attackers, they needed soldiers to protect it. They needed archers to rain down their arrows. They needed swordsmen on the battlements to fight off anyone who managed to scale the walls. Without all that, there was nothing to stop the Queen from invading and taking the castle as hers.

"So, she will take this castle," Bree said, tugging the leather belt around her waist, and slipping the dagger into the band. "And what will she do to all of the cursed fae when she does?"

Bree knew the answer to that question. She did not need Eurig to confirm the reality of this war, but she felt compelled to ask him anyway. She needed to hear him say it. She needed the reality of what was about to come to solidify itself in her mind. Because it would be what she needed to keep moving forward.

"She will either kill or imprison them, probably both." Eurig's expression hardened as he remembered everything his Queen had done to him as well. "Some she will deem useful to her, so she will lock them up in your dungeons. Others...she will not want around. Taveon, for one. Most if not all of the council members. And I cannot see her wanting to keep Rafe around either. He's too volatile, too loyal to the King."

Shivers coursed along Bree's skin. She needed to find that raven, and then she needed to warn Taveon of what was about to come. She still hadn't sent the information through the bond, knowing that he would only try to talk her out of bringing the raven back to life. Whatever he was scared him, and it scared Eurig, too. Bree had a feeling that she would understand that fear when she finally knew the full truth of him. But it was just one more raven. One more life she had to bring back. It was a life that could save the entire realm.

"Right. Well, I'm not going to let her take it that easily," Bree said with a nod, and crossed toward the open door. "I'm going to go get that raven. Don't try to stop me."

"I'm not going to try to stop you this time, Bree," Eurig said, a new determination hardening his voice. "I'm going with you, and I am going to help you. The Queen has no claim over this throne, and I will not let her have it. If that means you bringing back another creature, then so be it."

The Queen had done her best to beat him down, but she had failed. Eurig was stronger than he ever was, and she had made an enemy in him. An enemy that might very well end up being her undoing.

Bree and Eurig exited the hall and found the little patch of ground where Bree had buried the raven. She sank to her knees and dug until she found it, extracting the fragile creature from the dirt. She hoped it hadn't been too long. She hoped it wasn't too late. The curse had happened days ago, and there was no more warmth left underneath the dark feathers.

Bree closed her eyes and called to the brightness that sung through her veins. It sparked to life, that brilliant flame that licked her insides. It was brighter and harsher this day, the power so strong that she felt as if it might topple her to the ground. Bree dug her fingers into the dirt, one hand brushing against the bird's feathers.

In the back of her mind, she heard Taveon whispering into her ear. The walls had fallen between them now, despite her every urge to keep them up. It was the intensity of the power, she realized. It had knocked away everything else. She was the power, and the power was her. They had become one, and a spark of fear lit in her gut.

She was not sure she would be able to let it go, not this time.

"Bree," Taveon whispered, his voice insistent. "Bree, please stop. This is a terrible, terrible idea. It will end up killing you if you are not careful."

Bree shook her head against his words. The power could not kill her. It had made her immortal, just like Taveon. It did not take life away. It gave it.

Bree found every ounce of courage within her veins and she pushed the power down to her fingertips and into the cold bird. Her heart and soul felt torn in two as the magic ripped out of her body. Booms shook through her, and her eardrums popped in her head. Her vision went black, and the world went on mute.

Nothing existed but Bree and Bree alone. Without the power, she was nothing.

CHAPTER 26
EURIG

Bree collapsed onto the ground just as the raven spread its wings and soared away through the air, disappearing into nothing more than a black speck on the cobalt sky. Eurig dropped to his knees, fear churning through his gut. Bree was far stronger than he had first given her credit for, and she was fiercer than even the beast that lurked inside of her.

But she was still mortal, even with the bond she had with Taveon. And whatever she had just done was far too much for her frail body.

"Bree?" Eurig asked, taking her soft hand in his and bringing it to his lips. He had seen her do this before. Twice now. The first time, she had looked as though she was a little dizzy. The second, she breathed as though she'd just run a marathon. But now, something about this one was different. Her eyes had rolled back in her head and she had fallen heavily to the ground, just like all the other fae who had fallen in this castle.

Blinking back the tears in his eyes, Eurig slid his arms underneath her and lifted her from the ground. He would take her straight to Taveon. The King would be the first to wake from the curse, and he was the only one who could bring Bree back from whatever had happened.

Eurig had to act fast, pounding his feet against the stone floor as he flew down the hall toward Taveon's chambers. The King was already waiting for him when he arrived. His eyes were wide and his mouth was grim, and he took in Bree's state with such a look of dread that it made Eurig's bones go cold.

"You should not have let her do this." Taveon would not meet Eurig's eyes.

Eurig strode over to Taveon's bed and lowered Bree onto it. "You know how she is. There is no telling her not to do a damn thing once her mind is made up. If I had tried to stop her, she would have run away from me and she would have done it anyway."

"You did not tell her what I am," Taveon said, a statement more than a question. Because of course Taveon would know. The bond he had with Bree went far beyond anything Eurig could even imagine. They shared thoughts. And memories. And yet

Taveon had still managed to keep the truth hidden from her.

"I swore I would never tell a soul, and so I have not. But she deserves to know the truth, especially now. Your corrupted power has done something to her. Will you be able to heal her, Taveon?"

"I do not know."

CHAPTER 27

TAVEON

Taveon's heart had never hurt more than it did in that moment. This was all his fault. Bree's strange trance-like state was all because of him. Because she felt compelled to help him. Because he had been unable to help himself. And because he had been too afraid to tell her the truth about him.

But Taveon also knew that Bree would have gone through with it even if he had told her who and what he was. It would not have stopped her. She would have insisted on sacrificing herself to save the raven, to save him.

And now he would have to do the same in return.

Bree had not only brought him back, but she had saved his court as well. When the walls had collapsed between them, he had heard everything. And he had seen everything that had happened since she had closed herself off to him. An army of outposters was on the way, led by a desperate Queen willing to sacrifice every outposter life in order to get the power she had always craved. Taveon had always known that she would not stop at the outposts, that one day she would come for his throne.

And now that day had come.

Taveon knelt beside the bed and took Bree's hands in his. Oh, how things had changed. Only days ago, she had been the one comforting him while he had imagined the feel of her skin under his. He tried to talk to her through the bond, but only silence answered. Wherever she was and whatever had happened to her, it was not the same curse that had been cast upon him.

No, this was something else. This was all Taveon. A punishment for his power. A reminder of just how dangerous he could be.

Taveon closed his eyes and sent every ounce of his healing power toward Bree. He still felt weak from being stuck inside of his own mind for days. But he still managed to find every ounce of power he could.

Somewhere in the back of his mind, a warning sounded. A warning he had never heard before.

It knocked against the bond with a sharp blade, threatening to break his connection with Bree. His heart ached. Tears pricked his eyes. Even in the short weeks that he'd been so close to her, he had begun to depend on that connection he had with her. She liked to close herself off to him, but never completely. She was always there, inside of him and around him. She was in his soul, and he was in hers. And it was the kind of link that he never wanted to let go.

If you heal her, the tiny voice said, *it will break the bond between you. She has used a power no mortal should ever use. There must be payment in return.*

Taveon recognized the voice. He had heard it in his mind before, but it had been years. He had started to think that it was gone. He'd thought he'd managed to shake it off. But now it was back, slithering into his ears like the snake it was.

It broke Taveon's heart to let go of his connection to Bree. He doubted he would ever feel that close to anyone ever again, no matter how many centuries he might exist in this realm. But he would not let her die because of his own loneliness.

Taking a deep breath in through flared nostrils, Taveon poured all of his power into Bree's slack form. Pain shot through his core as the bond between them snapped in half. A cut that he knew was permanent. He would never again be able to hear her voice in his mind.

Emptiness consumed him.

CHAPTER 28

BREE

When Bree awoke, it felt as though she had a hole in her chest. She'd been dead to the world. She hadn't been able to hear or see or feel anything, but she knew exactly what had happened. In a burst of brilliant light, Bree had seen and heard everything. It was just a moment, a small snapshot in time, but it had been enough to fill in all of the blanks in her head.

She cracked open her eyes and stared up at Taveon. He was leaning over the bed with a grave expression on his face. The bond between them was no longer there, making her feel as if he were miles further away than he was.

"Hello, stranger," she whispered, blinking back the tears that arose from the sorrow she felt. She no longer had that inexplicable link to Taveon's mind, heart, and soul. She felt as though a part of her had been taken away, as if her soul had been ripped to shreds.

Taveon flicked his eyes to her face, and his entire body sighed in relief. "Thank the forest. I was scared it hadn't worked. Without the bond...my apologies. I am sure you had no idea what's happened. I'm afraid I have to tell you that…"

"I know." Bree gave him a smile. "I know everything, Taveon. In those last few moments when we were linked, everything came flooding into my mind. Everything I thought I'd forgotten."

She hoped that he understood what she meant, but he could no longer read her mind as he once had.

Taveon stiffened, and his hands tightened around the blanket spread across her body. "Everything? Does this mean you know…?"

Her heart hurt for him. He couldn't even bring himself to say the words aloud. Not that she could blame him. If she were him, she would never want a single soul to know either.

"I heard your thoughts. I read your memories. I know that you are not fully a Dark Fae."

Part Dark Fae, yes. But not fully. His mother *had* been King Midas's wife, but his father...well, he was something else entirely. Something that Bree had no idea even existed until Taveon's memories fluttered through her mind like pictures he had tried to burn.

"I was going to tell you, you know," Taveon said softly, grinding his teeth together. "I did not want you to discover it that way. I wanted to look into your eyes and explain it to you."

"So, explain it to me, Taveon. I'm all ears. Even though I have seen your memories, I would rather hear you tell it to me. In your own words. The way you wanted."

Taveon drew in a long, shuddering breath. His grip around her hand tightened, and Bree could read his every thought even if they were no longer bonded. She knew the truth of him now, and he was still scared to share the very darkest parts of himself.

"My mother...you know about her," Taveon began. "She was a good female. And she was loyal to King Midas. Unfortunately, he did not believe she stayed true to him. Not when she became pregnant with me, and I was not his son. But there is far more to the story than that."

Bree nodded, squeezing his hand in comfort.

He continued, "There is another realm, though many do not know of it. Centuries and centuries ago, this knowledge was passed on from mother to daughter and father to son, but somewhere along the way, we let ourselves forget it. This realm may be called Underworld, but there is another realm far darker than ours. It is the Realm of the Dead, and it is ruled by far worse creatures than those found here. Demonic gods. Males and females full of violence and terror. And death."

Bree shivered at his words, and she couldn't help

but feel a spark of terror in her gut. The fae in the Light Fae realm had always spoken of Underworld in hushed tones of fear. They said the Dark Fae were chaotic and evil, and while some were that way, Bree had realized that the Light Fae had been wrong.

But maybe they never had been wrong. Not truly. Maybe they had always been talking about another realm, one far worse than this one.

"The gates between our realm and their realm are shut, but it has not always been that way. We are safe from them now, as are the Light Fae, and as are the humans. Somehow though, one got through. One of the demonic gods."

Taveon's voice broke off, and Bree's heart hurt for him. She knew what he would say next. She wished she could take that burden from him. But now that he had begun speaking, it was as if the dam had broken within him, and the words were spilling out from his soul. He needed to tell his story now.

"He found my mother, the wife of the Dark Fae's King. And then he raped her." Taveon's grip tightened around her hand, and he was clinging on to her so tightly that it almost hurt. But she just let him hold her, knowing that he needed to feel something solid underneath his fingertips. "I am his offspring. I am part Dark Fae, but I am also part demonic god. And I've never been able to ask him why he did this. As soon as he got what he wanted, he was gone and no one from the Realm of the Dead has been seen since. Unless you count me."

"Of course I don't count you, Taveon," Bree said as gently as she could. "You may be part demonic god, but your soul and your heart is all fae. You are a good male, Taveon. There is nothing evil about you. You are kind, you're generous, and you are brave. You care about this realm, and you care about the humans, even though none of the other Dark Fae could give a damn."

The grip on her hand loosened, and Taveon finally met her eyes. His own were full of unshed tears and pain that echoed years of torment. This was a burden he had carried around with him all this time, like a noose slid tightly around his neck. She wished there was something she could say or do to make that pain go away, but all she could do was accept him for exactly who he was. Her king. Her Taveon.

Taveon wanted to insist that she rest, but Bree was back on her feet within hours. There was an army of outposters outside of their gates, probably readying themselves to attack at any moment. The other court members had started to wake up, and they needed to gather everyone together in the Great Hall and tell them exactly what was coming. They needed to plan. They needed soldiers. And they needed to gather as many weapons as they could.

Rafe found her exiting Taveon's chambers, and his arms wrapped around her so tight that her breath was knocked from her lungs. Relief poured through her, and she snaked her arms around his back, squeezing him just as tightly as he squeezed her.

He pulled back, searched her face with those silver eyes of his, and pressed her hair back away from her face. His lips hungrily found hers, rough and soft at the same time. When he pulled back, Bree was left gasping for more, and a delicious heat rolled through her stomach.

"I really, really wish an army of angry outposters was not two seconds away from attacking this castle," Bree whispered, leaning into him and breathing him in.

"Oh, Bree, you have no idea. I feel as if I have not seen you for years. I cannot even explain it. It was if I was awake, alive inside of the darkness. But I could not hear a thing. I could not see a thing. The only image I had was your face, your smile, and those eyes of yours. It was the only thing that kept me going and knowing that everything would turn out okay."

His words warmed Bree from her head all the way down to her toes. He was here before her now, and there was something she yearned to whisper into his ears. Why, oh why, did they have to prepare for a battle right now? Why could she not take him back to her room and show him exactly everything she felt inside of her heart?

"Soon," she whispered.

He gave a nod. "If we survive this."

"When," Bree insisted. "Not if."

❧

Every single fae who had shown for Taveon's celebration had gathered in the Great Hall for the meeting about the upcoming battle. Murmurs, angry ones, rippled through the crowd like choppy waves at sea. Every single fae who had fallen was now alive and well and awake. But they were angry. The outposters had attacked them in their own home, they had targeted their new King, and their vengeance was in desperate need of release.

Dagen stood on the stage beside Taveon with Conlan, Branok, and Ethne just behind them. Their faces were solemn, but their eyes were full of fire. They were just as angry as the crowd before them.

"Thank you all for gathering here, even after the confusion of this morning. I know some of you have questions." Taveon raised his voice to be heard over the entire crowd, and the murmurs fell to silence. With an outward force threatening their home, all of the inner turmoil whispered away into nothing. They were now loyal to their King, no matter whose son he wasn't.

One small, young male at the front of the crowd stood from his seat. "May I speak, my King?"

Taveon pursed his lips and gave a nod. "Of course. Every single member of my Court has a voice, including you."

"How will we beat them?" he asked. "What if they just try to curse all of us again?"

"We will have the element of surprise on our side," Taveon said with a nod. "They have no way of knowing that we are all un-cursed inside of this castle. They will be expecting nothing more than Eurig and Bree here. That will give us a chance to surround them before they can get inside our walls."

Bree raised her eyebrows. This was certainly not what she had expected. And by the sound of the murmuring voices, the rest of the Court had not expected it either. The castle was so heavily fortified, the perfect defensive system against potential invaders. The smart thing to do would be to hunker down inside, letting the soldiers take charge of the walls.

Taveon raised his hands in the air and gave the court a long serious look. They fell silent, listening to their King for once. "I understand your confusion and your wariness. And, in any other situation, I would agree. Our strength is in our walls. Our castle can protect us. But we have a chance here to take them out before they try to get inside and realize that none of us are cursed at all. They do not know we are in here. And we will use that to our advantage."

Across the room, Taveon turned his eyes her way, and he motioned for her to join him on the stage. Bree's face warmed as she stood from her seat, her feet moving as if she was in a trance. Every eye in the great hall was on her, and more murmurs filled the air. Bree had no idea what Taveon would ask of her, but she knew she would do it no matter what.

She joined him on the stage, and he placed a solid hand on her shoulder. "You all know my champion, Bree. Your freedom from the curse is all thanks to her. She found a way to undo it, and she may just be our saving grace in this fight." Her King turned toward her, his eyes solemn and his lips pressed tightly together. Her heart clenched tight. She wished that she could feel his emotions, just as she used to do. He felt so far away from her now, almost like a stranger. Almost like a King too far above everyone to truly know him.

But she did know him. Better than anyone else. And she trusted him not only with her body but with her heart.

"Bree, there is one last thing that I need for you to do." His eyes gazed deeply into hers, and she swore she could almost feel the whisper of his mind against hers. "We need you and Eurig to create a distraction. Can you do that for us?"

It was a question that she did not need to answer

because he knew what she would say. That was why he had brought her up before all of his Court without warning her. She would say yes. She would have volunteered even if he hadn't asked her. Because even though she was a stranger, a foreigner to these lands...somehow, over the past few months, this Court had become her home.

CHAPTER 29
BREE

Eurig and Bree crept out through the sewers. It had been the outposter's idea, and she'd wanted to smack him as soon as the words whispered from his lips. The tunnels stunk to high heaven, and she knew the smell would cling to her skin long after they'd exited into the fresh air.

When they reached the small hole in the side of the castle walls, they ducked down and pressed their backs against the stone that encircled the entire castle. In the distance, Bree could see the approaching army. There were hundreds of them, just like Eurig had warned. And they were riding straight toward the castle wall with no abandon. Because Taveon had also been right. They had no idea they would come up against any kind of force. They thought they would be able to ride straight inside and take the castle as their own.

"Too bad we have to be the bait instead of taking up our own weapons against them," Bree muttered as she glared at the fae who were responsible for everything that had happened. "I'd like to show them exactly where they can shove it."

Eurig chuckled. "I'm sure that you'll get plenty of chances to harass the Queen when she is behind bars in Taveon's dungeons."

That was another thing that Taveon had insisted upon. He wanted the Queen taken alive, and he wanted no shots fired her way. She was to be his prisoner, just like Eurig had been hers for so many years. It was the best and only way to keep the peace between his Court and the outposters when all of this was over. Otherwise, another army of angry outposters might charge their way.

"It's almost time," Eurig said, shifting his body closer to Bree. The scent of him enveloped her like a warm blanket. Mint and cinnamon and the sea. She leaned toward him and wrapped her arms around his neck, tipping back her head to stare into his angular face. Emotions battled inside of her chest. Fear and anger at the outposters clashed with the affection she felt toward this male.

"You ready?" Bree asked, heart practically in her throat.

Eurig gave a nod, they clasped hands, and then they pressed their foreheads together. With a deep collective breath, they both turned toward the charging fae.

A heavy hand slammed down hard on Bree's shoulder, and sharp fingernails dug into her skin. The hand yanked her back, and then pushed her to the ground where all of the breath was knocked from her lungs.

"Not so fast, Redcap girl." A tall, thin fae stood over her, sneering down at Bree while her dark reddish hair whipped around her sunken face. "Nor you, Eurig, though I can hardly believe my eyes. You're a traitor."

"I was banished," Eurig said through clenched teeth. "For having the King's blood running through my veins. That hardly makes me a traitor."

"No matter," another fae said. This one was male, and he had his arms wrapped tight around Eurig's chest. And, somehow, he was much larger than her outposter male. His grip was strong and sure, and Eurig wasn't going anywhere.

"Let us go," Bree said, though she knew it was useless. These were outposters, and they had caught them off guard. Bree stared helplessly at the approaching army. She and Eurig needed to be storming straight at them right now, or else they wouldn't be distracted enough for Taveon's soldiers to catch them unaware.

"The Queen will decide what to do with you," the

female said, yanking Bree hard from the ground and shoving her forward.

They met the approaching army in the middle of the field. Bree's jaws hurt from how hard she ground her teeth together, and her heart felt like a jackhammer in her chest. Eurig had gone silent while the fae shoved him along, and now more than ever, she wished she could read his thoughts. They needed to figure out a way to get out of this. They needed to find a way to turn this right back onto the outposters themselves.

The Queen rode at the front of her army, jet black hair trailing behind her. Her eyes were pinched and her jawline sharp, and there was something horribly unnerving about the female. She was tall and lithe like Bree's captor. Very unlike Eurig and most of the soldiers that surrounded their Queen.

She slowed her horse and held up her hand. The entire army shuddered to a stop in unison. Bree couldn't help but shiver.

The Queen elegantly slid off her horse, and her dainty feet hit the ground. She eyed Bree from head to toe, no emotions flickering in her dark eyes. "So, this is the King's champion. She is much plainer than I expected."

Bree ground her teeth together even harder, but she refused to rise to the Queen's bait. She would not say a word, no matter how hard the Queen tried to needle her.

The female's dark eyes flicked to Eurig, and a strange emotion flashed within the depths of them. It had been the only sign that she was not a robot, as far as Bree could tell.

"Eurig." She let out a sigh and shook her head. "Your father would be very disappointed if he knew you had joined the enemy."

Eurig spat on the ground by her feet. "I think he'd be a hell of a lot more likely to cheer me on. Or have you already forgotten that you *murdered* him?"

Several of the soldiers grunted in response. Their horses shifted underneath them, hooves stomping the dusty ground. Bree stared up at them all, silently demanding they explain themselves. How could they follow this Queen after what she had done? Why didn't they revolt against her rule?

But the Queen had no reaction to their mutterings. Instead, she turned toward the female who still held a tight grip on Bree and motioned for her to let go.

"I am growing impatient. Give her to me so we can put an end to this reign once and for all." The Queen's voice was full of ice and a raw kind of power that made Bree's bones ache from dread.

The female shoved Bree toward the Queen, and there was a sweet, sweet moment of pure freedom. Bree focused her thoughts on the beast within. The Queen could try whatever she liked, but she would be no match for the wolf. It raged inside of her, its insides desperate for a taste of the Queen's blood. And for once, Bree would give in to whatever the beast desired.

She gritted her teeth and forced her limbs to shift, but...nothing happened.

She focused on her hands, on her claws. They didn't come to her.

Frustration churned through her, tears pricking her eyes. What the hell was happening? Why wouldn't her beast respond? She could feel it inside of her, pacing and roaring and hungry for blood. Why would it not come out?

The Queen let out a light laugh, one that whispered away on the cool wind. "You must think I am an amateur, and you must be wondering why you cannot shift." She leaned down and hissed into Bree's face, her breath smelling like iron and salt. "I brought a Hawkborn with me. It will not allow you to shift in my presence."

Shit, Bree thought. So much for that bright idea.

And, unfortunately, it also meant that Bree was completely out of bright ideas now.

The Queen wrapped her icy hands around Bree's wrists and yanked her to her feet. She was surprisingly strong, and her grip was so tight that it made Bree's hands begin to tingle in response.

Dropping back her head, the Queen called out toward the gates of the castle that looked as silent and as still as a graveyard. "King Taveon. I have your champion, and I have your newest recruit. Surrender your Court and your castle to me or I *will* kill them both."

Bree's heart thundered hard. If only Taveon hadn't been forced to break the bond between them, Bree could communicate her plans to him. And she could use his power as her own. She could try to free Eurig and sacrifice herself to the Queen. She wouldn't know about the immortality.

The Queen waited, and silence rained down all around them.

Bree sniffed and gave the Queen a wicked smile. "You're barking up the wrong tree here. The King is...indisposed. I thought you knew that though. Or did someone else come up with that clever curse thing?"

The Queen's eyes glittered, and she did not deem it necessary to give Bree even the slightest of glances. "Do not play coy. I know that you were somehow able to reverse the curse I put on these fae. And the villagers. And the Wilde Fae. The King is very much awake, and he is watching us."

Shivers coursed along Bree's skin. So much for that approach.

After several more moments of brutal silence, the Queen wrapped one hand around Bree's throat and dug her sharp fingernails into her skin. Bree swallowed hard, and sparks dotted her vision. As much as Bree did not want Taveon to succumb to this

Queen, she also knew exactly what this meant for her life.

The Queen would not hesitate to kill her. She was not bluffing. If Taveon did not surrender, Bree was dead.

Bree closed her eyes, letting her mind replay every moment of her life. From her childhood spent exploring the Manhattan streets with Norah, to the moment when she'd been infected by the Redcap virus and she'd fled to the safety of the Light Fae realm. To the moment when she'd passed through that Faerie Ring and into Underworld. Knowing Rafe. Knowing Taveon. Knowing Dagen. Knowing Eurig.

Both the good and the bad, she cherished.

"This is my last warning, King Taveon," the Queen called out, the screech in her voice betraying her calm and collected exterior. "Surrender. Or she dies this night."

In the distance, Bree heard the unmistakable clank of the iron gates opening wide.

No, her mind raged. *Stop!*

Her eyes flew open, and Bree spotted Taveon's tall and commanding form striding through the open gates, his hands held up as if in surrender.

He couldn't. Taveon could not surrender his crown and his court to this monster. She would kill them all. She would tear every last one of the fae to shreds. And she wouldn't stop there. There was greed in the Queen's eyes. She would not be satisfied until she sat on every single throne she could. And that included far more than just those found in this realm.

Taveon strode closer, and Bree's heart ran wild. Her eyes flicked to Eurig who stared down at the ground in defeat. The Hawkborn would prevent her from shifting, but there had to be something else she could do.

The dagger, a little voice whispered into her mind. Dagen's dagger.

She'd shoved it into the little hidden folds of the Dark Fae fighting leathers when she'd been forced to change into a new set of clothes. It was right there, just within her reach. If she was quick enough...

Without giving her mind a chance to talk herself out of it, Bree shoved her hand into her leathers, wrapped her fingers around the golden hilt, and then whirled toward the Queen. The blade found its mark, sinking into the Queen's forehead with a sickening crunch.

Bree's hands flew to her mouth, and she stumbled back. Horror churned through her gut. Blood poured from the wound, pooling around the hilt that protruded from the Queen's head. The female's eyes went round, and then she fell straight back, slamming hard against the ground.

Shouts exploded all around her and rough hands grabbed her arms. The soldiers leapt from their horses, surrounding both Eurig and Bree. Their faces were screwed up in anger, though others looked jubilant and surprised. Every sword was raised, and every bow was drawn. And Bree had no idea who was pointing at who, and who was pointing at her.

"Let me go," Eurig said, his voice as clear as the moonlit sky. "I am Eurig, son of Clarke, and I demand that you let me go."

The fae who held him dropped his grip and stepped back, and several of the outposters fell to the ground on their knees, bowing before him.

"Let her go, too," he said to the half a dozen outposters who had surrounded Bree.

"Eurig," one of the males said, frowning. "She stabbed our Queen."

"Let her go," he said again. He stood tall before them, his presence commanding and full of power. It was a side to him he'd never shown Bree, and she almost felt compelled to fall to her knees as well.

The fae let her go, but they did not disperse from around her. They still hung in close, eyeing her with a wariness that made Bree's head spin. She hadn't really thought things through. Killing the Queen had seemed like the best idea in the world, but only if the outposters hated her.

And it appeared they didn't. Or, at least some of them didn't.

Eurig took a step in close to her and dropped his voice to a low whisper. "There is something I must do, Bree. It is the only way to save us both. I...I will miss you."

Those last few words were so low that Bree couldn't be sure she'd actually heard them. And then he stepped back, putting as much distance between them as he could. He turned toward the outposters, looking each one in the eye.

"She killed the Queen!" one shouted.

Another outposter dropped back his head and yelled, "We must avenge her death! Down with Taveon's court!"

Eurig held up a hand. "There will be no avenging. There will be no retaliation. I am Eurig, bastard son of Clarke, and I present myself to you as your future King. And my first order to you is this: I will lead us back to our lands, and we will spill no more blood here this night."

EPILOGUE

BREE

Bree sat in the balcony of the highest tower, staring glumly out at the setting moon. It had been more than a week since the outposters had tried to take control of Taveon's castle, but she hadn't been able to celebrate their win.

Rafe eased in behind her, settling onto the stone perch that jutted out over the top of the Keep. "I thought I might find you here."

Bree hugged her knees to her chest and sighed. "Am I that predictable?"

"No. You're not." He elbowed her in the side and smiled. "But your emotions are written all over your face, Bree. You miss him."

Every part of her heart felt broken into pieces. She not only missed him, but she felt betrayed. He was supposed to stay with her, he was supposed to fight by her side. Instead, he'd abandoned her the moment he had the chance to grasp his crown. She remembered having asked him if he wanted to go back home, and he'd said no.

She felt like an idiot for believing him.

"Missing him would mean that I actually want to see him again," Bree muttered.

"He did what he had to do, and you know it," Rafferty said. "If he didn't take charge, they would have killed you and then swarmed the gates of the castle. And they probably would have killed half of their own while they were at it. Some of them wanted to crown you Queen for what you did, and some of them wanted to rip you to shreds. It would have only ended in chaos."

Her heart squeezed tight. "But he didn't even say goodbye. He just left. He didn't even cast a glance over his shoulder when he walked away."

"Probably because he could not bear to see the look on your face," Rafe said with a sigh. "Listen, Bree. Eurig is not my favorite fae in this realm. We have had our differences, do not forget. All that said, there is no denying that he would do anything for Taveon. And, I daresay, anything for you. He did not take the crown because he wants power. He took it because he saw no other way."

"Maybe. Maybe not." Tears sprung into her eyes and then leaked out onto her cheeks. "Either way, I'll never get to see him again."

Rafferty gave her a sad smile. "Then, I suppose you are just stuck with me."

Bree caught his glance, and the hardness around her heart softened. She could not be sad with Rafe by her side. Yes, she would always miss Eurig. They had shared something between them that she would never forget, no matter if he ruled the outposts or not.

"I brought something for you," he said, reaching into a rucksack that Bree had not noticed until now. With a soft smile, he pulled her old fighting leathers out of the bag. Bree's eyes widened. How had he managed that? They'd been torn to shreds. She'd left the pieces of them behind on the rolling hills.

Bree reached out and fingered the soft material. Those were her leathers through and through. "How?"

"Taveon told me what happened and how upset you were about losing them, so I found the scraps and asked one of our best seamstresses to mend them for you," Rafe said, pressing his lips together into a thin line. "I know they're important to you. They're your link back to your home."

Bree glanced up and smiled at him, the sadness in her heart replaced with something else. Love. "Thank you for this, Rafe, but you know what? Why don't you hold on to them for now?"

Confusion rippled across his handsome features. "I don't understand."

"This is my home now, Rafe. Here with you and Taveon. I don't need my old fighting leathers to remind me of who I once was anymore." She rested her hand on top of his and squeezed tight. "Besides, I have new fighting leathers now. Ones that I have to admit fit me much better than the old ones ever did."

And she had Rafe. Her sexy, smart, strong, and kindhearted Rafe. Smiling, she leaned into him and pressed her lips tight against his. Everything would be okay as long as she had Rafe.

※

Back in her quarters, she began to pack her things together. She would move back into Rafe's rooms now. He and Taveon had told her that they had redecorated it somehow, and she couldn't wait to see what they'd been up to. It was good timing. After Eurig's retreat, she did not want to sleep alone anymore. It only reminded her that he'd left.

But things were looking up. The Court was finally starting to get back to normal, and Taveon had begun to rule his people with the kindness and thoughtfulness he'd always promised. And, Bree had to admit, he looked damn good on the throne. Like he belonged there.

A knock sounded on the door, and she turned toward it with a smile, expecting Rafe or Taveon.

Instead, it was Fillan.

Her stomach dropped. She'd forgotten all about the assassin and his demand that she find out Taveon's secret.

Now that she knew it, she wanted to do nothing but run.

"Get out," she said in a sharp voice. "You're not welcome here."

Fillan raised his eyebrows and stepped inside her room, closing the door behind him.

She crossed her arms over her chest. "I said get out."

"Why the sudden change in attitude toward me?" he asked with a frown. "I thought you would be pleased to find that I am awake and free of that horrible curse."

She raised an eyebrow. "That curse actually affected you?"

"It did," he said with a solemn nod. "I hear you are to thank for freeing us all from it. Tell me, Bree, how did you do it?"

Bree's heart thumped hard. She refused to tell the assassin what she'd done. There was no doubt in her mind that he would put two and two together, figuring out once and for all what Taveon was hiding from the realm. And she couldn't let him do that.

"A little bird told me the trick," she merely said, half-smiling at her play on words.

Fillan furrowed his eyebrows and stepped

forward. "Bree. This is serious. How did you undo the curse? Did it have anything to do with what Taveon is?"

All the blood drained from Bree's face. "No."

"Bree," he said again, tucking a finger underneath her chin and forcing her to look up into his eyes. "Listen to me. If I am right about Taveon's true nature, then this entire realm is in danger."

Frowning, Bree tried to jerk away, but his finger held her firmly in place. "What are you talking about?"

"The demonic gods," Fillan said in a low growl. "They are trying to find a way to break open the gates so they can come and take back their son."

ALSO BY JENNA WOLFHART

REVERSE HAREM FANTASY

Otherworld Academy

A Dance with Darkness

A Song of Shadows

A Touch of Starlight

A Cage of Moonlight

A Heart of Midnight

A Throne of Illusions

Protectors of Magic

Wings of Stone

Carved in Stone

Bound by Stone

Shadows of Stone

ROMANTIC EPIC FANTASY

The Fallen Fae

Court of Ruins

Prince of Shadows (A Novella)

Kingdom in Exile

Keeper of Storms

PARANORMAL ROMANCE

The Paranormal PI Files

Live Fae or Die Trying

Dead Fae Walking

Bad Fae Rising

One Fae in the Grave

Innocent Until Proven Fae

All's Fae in Love and War

The Supernatural Spy Files

Confessions of a Dangerous Fae

Confessions of a Wicked Fae

The Bone Coven Chronicles

Witch's Curse

Witch's Storm

Witch's Blade

Witch's Fury

ABOUT THE AUTHOR

Jenna Wolfhart spends her days tucked away in her writing shed filled with books and plants. When she's not writing, she loves to deadlift, rewatch Game of Thrones, and drink copious amounts of coffee.

Born and raised in America, Jenna now lives in England with her husband, her two dogs, and her mischief of rats.

www.jennawolfhart.com
jenna@jennawolfhart.com

Printed in Great Britain
by Amazon